THE BLACK MOUNTAIN DUTCHMAN

In Wyoming, when Maggie Buckner is captured by a gang of outlaws, 'the Dutchman' is the only one who can free her. Near Savage Peak, the old man adjusts the sights on his Remington No. 1 rifle as the riders come into range. When he stops shooting, three of the captors lay dead. After striking the first deadly blows, the Dutchman trails the group across South Pass like the fourth horseman of the apocalypse ... and surely Hell follows with him.

STEVE RITCHIE

THE BLACK MOUNTAIN DUTCHMAN

Complete and Unabridged

LINFORD
Leicester

First published in Great Britain in 2010 by
Robert Hale Limited
London

First Linford Edition
published 2012
by arrangement with
Robert Hale Limited
London

The moral right of the author has been asserted

British Library CIP Data

Ritchie, Steve.
  The Black Mountain Dutchman.- -
  (Linford western library)
  1. Western stories.
  2. Large type books.
  I. Title II. Series
  823.9'2–dc23

  ISBN 978–1–4448–0952–7

Published by
F. A. Thorpe (Publishing)
Anstey, Leicestershire
Set by Words & Graphics Ltd.
Anstey, Leicestershire
Printed and bound in Great Britain by
T.J. International Ltd., Padstow, Cornwall

This book is printed on acid-free paper

I would like to dedicate my first published work to the man who most inspired me to become a writer, Dr Woodridge Spears PhD. Dr Spears, this one's for you.

1

And I looked, and behold a pale horse: and his name that sat on him was Death, and Hell followed with him.

Revelation 6:8

The tall grulla gelding stood in a small aspen grove at the edge of a bench, his dark head up, listening with his black-tipped ears pricked forward. He stood on a point west of Savage Peak, some 1,000 feet above the prairie floor. Scattered throughout the grove were large slabs of rock which had been shoved up through the earth's surface thousands, maybe even millions, of years before. His pale-bluish roan color with its contrasting darker markings allowed him to blend into the rocks near which he stood, making him nearly invisible from a distance. Twice he shook his dark head to rid himself of a

1

pesky fly that buzzed about his ears.

The old man who sat atop the grulla was looking through his long-glass. From his vantage point on the narrow bench he was watching the short column of riders who rode on the prairie floor below, still nearly four miles south-east of where he now sat his horse.

'Stand still, Buster,' the old man demanded of the horse.

He was having trouble staying focused on the group. Eventually he stepped down, trailed the reins, and walked to the nearest slab of rock. He leaned against the huge granite slab and looked again.

For half an hour he watched as the group rode closer, making certain as to the path they would take. Then the old man mounted once more and rode slowly down the mountainside, staying to the cover of the thick aspens and pines as well as the boulders and large slabs of granite, to a similar position as he had before. Here he would have a clear field of fire for nearly a mile. The ground that lay before him was relatively flat with little cover and, although there was a steady breeze, it would be a tailwind and should not affect the flight of his bullets, even at such a long range.

He recalled having a similar layout on several occasions, when fighting hostile Indians since coming to the West, and as a youngster in the mountains of Tennessee. He had planned many battles and had killed his share of men in his fifty-plus years; it had been kill or be killed, whether in military skirmishes, personal feuds or Indian fighting. But what he planned now was nothing short of cold-blooded murder . . . but he reckoned that he could live with it.

The eight riders drew nearer, now; he estimated the range to be three-quarters of a mile. There was a bandoleer filled with hand-loaded .45.70 cartridges lying close at hand and three more rounds were held between the fingers of his left hand, which also held the fore-stock of his rifle. His shooting station being ready, the old man rested the Remington No 1 Rifle on an aspen log and made himself comfortable.

He rested his cheek on the aged persimmon stock, then, with an expert's touch, he adjusted the tang rear sight, setting it for the appropriate distance. When the group had closed the distance between them to what he estimated to be 800 yards, he thumbed back the hammer, aimed at the man at the head of the short column and gently placed his finger on the trigger.

The eight riders had emerged from the Granite Mountains north of Devil's Gate and then ridden out onto the rolling, open prairie, unaware that the old man waited and watched them from his shooting station high up on the rocky table. There was little talk among them as the old man aligned the sights of the single-shot rifle. Ben Anderson, who rode at the front of the column leading the way for the small group, had just suggested to his cousin, Alvin

Harding, who was riding second in line, that they should stop for the night along the banks of Sheep Creek, at the base of Sheep Mountain. As Ben had stated his opinion, the old man slowly took up the slack in the trigger.

Harding had just acknowledged Ben's suggestion when all of the riders heard an eerie, sickening *thud*. Ben suddenly pitched backward and to the left in his saddle and fell to the ground; nearly three seconds later they heard the distant, heavy *boom* of the rifle.

The small caravan halted in their tracks, the remaining seven riders staring in shock at the bloody, dead man who lay on the ground. Alvin was turning to warn the others to scatter when they heard a similar *thud* as before. As the report of the rifle sounded for the second time, young Tom Ferguson had already been lifted from his saddle by the impact of the bullet and lay sprawled on the ground, the fresh green shoots of buffalo grass beneath him turning red with his blood.

'Scatter!' Alvin yelled frantically. 'We'll meet up at the place where Ben said we'd make camp.' Then he pointed and added quickly, 'Just ride toward the end of those mountains to the south.'

Having given them their orders, he jerked the reins of the bay upon which Maggie Buckner rode and spurred his mount to the south-west in the direction of Muddy Gap. His brother Arnold and Tom's younger brother, Sam, reined their horses to the south and were ready to hightail it across the Sweetwater when they heard the unnerving *thud* once more.

Arnold turned in his saddle to see whom else they had lost and saw Charlie Emerson grasping the blood-soaked front of his coat. His cold lifeless eyes stared back at Arnold as he rolled forward and fell from his saddle. Jim Emerson yelled, 'Move, boys,' as he raced past and Arnold sank his spurs into the flanks of his mount. As the horse leapt forward he heard a *whoosh* and then the *whack* and *whine* of a spent bullet ricocheting off of a nearby rock and the eventual heavy report of the rifle.

They had no idea from whence the shots had come. The only thought in the minds of all three men was to get out of range of that big gun. Within minutes, Arnold, Jim and Sam were across the Sweetwater and riding hard for the cover of a nearby wash, *en route* to the mountains south of where they now rode. Alvin, who was leading the bay on which the girl rode, had disappeared somewhere among the cottonwoods that grew along the banks of the river and was nowhere to be seen.

They were over a mile south of the Sweetwater and had slowed their pace when Sam turned to Arnold and said, 'We told Alvin that girl was gonna be nothing but trouble.'

'Not now, Sam,' Arnold snarled. 'We've got bigger problems. We don't know this country like that old man does. We've gotta find Alvin and make

7

up some kind of plan to kill that old coot.'

'Hang that,' Sam insisted. 'My brother's lying back there with a hole the size of a cantaloupe plumb through him.'

'Yeah. He's dead and we're not.' Then nothing else was said. They rode for over three hours before crossing the creek nearest the end of the mountain range toward which Alvin had pointed. It was nearly an hour after that when they saw the two horses picketed near the water at the base of what they guessed to be Sheep Mountain.

The three men dismounted, stripped the gear from their horses and picketed them with the two which were already there. Then they walked to the fire, where Alvin was chewing on a strip of jerked beef. 'All things considered, ain't that fire a bit chancy?' Sam asked. Alvin only flashed a sadistic gaze in his direction.

Suddenly, Arnold remembered that Tom had been leading their pack horse and that no one had taken the time to grab the lead rope as they had fled. 'We don't have any food?'

With his teeth clenched in anger Alvin shook his head. 'I guess not. I had hold of the lead rope on the horse she was on. I guess I just figured that one of you would have had sense enough to pick up the pack horse.' He bit into the jerky, ripped off another bite then added, 'Don't worry about it. We'll get another horse and supplies in South Pass City. We should get there sometime tomorrow, I guess.' He was utterly disgusted with the entire situation when he asked sarcastically, 'One of you know anything at all about this country? Ben was the only one of us who had ever been through here before. All I know is what I've been told about it . . . strictly hearsay.' All three of the young men shook their heads in reply, to which Alvin grunted his disgust.

Alvin Harding was their leader and had always displayed an air of confidence, as long as Ben had been around to guide them. But now he was alone,

9

or nearly so, and his mind was racing. Ben was dead, he was certain of that. He had seen a large ugly wound where the bullet, which had passed through the man's body, had exited from the middle of his back. Tom Ferguson had suffered an identical wound; he had not known about Charlie Emerson until Arnold's group had ridden into the camp.

Four of his group were now dead and the most important member of the group — his guide — was among them. Now he could only hope that between those who remained, they could remember enough of what they had been told to allow them to find their way to South Pass City, or perhaps Green River, Harding thought suddenly. The old man might not think to look for them in that direction until, perhaps, they were already out of the country.

Harding then gave thought to the girl. It was by sheer luck that they had found her. Then there had been the shooting. Kevin Love and the Emerson brothers had seen their share of shooting scrapes but neither Arnold nor Sam had ever been involved in any sort of gun play until they had ganged up on that old Indian at the store near the bridge at Casper.

As they had walked their horses down the dusty street of the growing little settlement, they had seen the girl entering the mercantile; she had been accompanied by the old Indian, of whom he had heard. Ben Anderson had been sent to locate and retrieve the girl's horse while the rest of the group had waited on the street for them to exit the store. As the girl and her companion had stepped from the building onto the street, the members of the group had approached from different directions. Ben was already leading her mount down the street as Alvin had grabbed the girl and informed her that she was coming with him; the Indian had instinctively reached for his side-arm. Several shots rang out and the old Sioux warrior lay on the ground.

Even while shots were still being fired, Alvin had quickly lifted the girl and swung her into her saddle, then he and one of his men had tied her feet in the stirrups with piggin strings. The entire incident had taken place in such a short period of time that none of the by-standers had been able to offer any interference. With shots being fired at them from across the river at the edge of town, the nine riders had fled the settlement in a cloud of dust, riding westward along the North Platte River.

Alvin Harding had finally located and regained that which he owned . . . his property, Maggie Buckner.

★   ★   ★

The old man watched the fleeing riders for some time, then he slung the bandoleer over his shoulder, picked up his empty brass and walked back to the grulla. He mounted and rode from the table, down the mountain and out onto the open prairie to where the three dead men lay. He checked each man, saw that they were indeed finished, then gathered the horses that had been left behind when the remaining five riders had fled, one of which was their pack horse. He suddenly realized that they were now without supplies . . . and the old man's lips formed a wry smile.

As he stripped the gear from the deserted riding stock, he gave thought to where Harding would lead his diminished group of greenhorns. They had retreated in the direction of the Green Mountains which comprise the extreme western end of the Sweetwater Range. There, they could find plenty of water and, with some luck, game for camp meat if they dared take a shot. But for now they had no supplies: no coffee, no salt, no beans or bacon.

Their original route would have taken them to Fort Bridger, where Alvin Harding would have replenished his food stores. Now, he might consider another route. South Pass would be the closest town where he could purchase supplies, but Green River was nearly as close and would be a wiser choice. The old man had to think.

Once the gear had been removed from the abandoned horses, he pulled their shoes, then turned them loose. They would fare well here, for there was grass and water enough for them. Eventually, they would likely join a wild herd, wander into the closest stage relay station, or be found by one of the few local ranchers. He had heard of a cattle spread east of his current location, somewhere just west of the Pedros near the confluence of the Sweetwater and North Platte.

As the freed horses walked away and began to graze the old man stripped the dead men of their gunbelts and searched them for any valuables. He took a few gold coins from all three, a gold watch from the pocket of his first victim and a pair of ornate silver spurs from the boots of one of the others. Once he had removed the rifles from the dead men's saddle scabbards, he tied the extra weapons on the pack-horse, mounted the grulla and then rode south, following the trail left by Harding and the girl. Anyone could have recognized immediately that Harding was certainly a greenhorn, because it was an easy trail to follow.

He was still an hour's ride north of Sheep Mountain when he reined the grulla away from the trail left by the two riders and entered a small grove of cottonwoods that grew along Sheep Creek. There he stripped the animals of their gear, then, in a depression near the edge of the creek where he would be concealed, he built a small fire and set his coffee pot at its edge.

After seeing to the horses, he sipped his coffee as he prepared his supper, all the while thinking of what he must do to free the girl . . . safely. He had no doubt that it would mean the killing of the remaining four men. Alvin Harding had known where to find her, so the old man must assume that the man had gained information about the two men with whom she had stayed after eluding him. If Harding had gained any knowledge of him, he would be certain that the old man would never cease his pursuit until his objective was reached; his feudal history and military background would be evidence enough of that.

The old man's first thought, however, must be of their new route, if indeed Harding changed it. He had no idea as to the man's knowledge of the country. Had he been this way before? Did any of the remaining men know their intended route? Over the past two days since they had fled Casper, he had observed the group and was certain that the first man he had shot knew the country; he had been at the head of the short column when they had emerged from the Granites. Although their trail had wandered a bit, that man had shown by the decisions he had made that he was a capable woodsman. The old man was certain that he was the same man who had tracked the girl when he and Antelope Horn had first seen the group on the prairie east of Big Mountain; thus he had made the decision to take that man with his first shot.

Having eaten his supper, the old man sat near the small fire. He fetched a small tin from the pocket of his capote, took a pinch of snuff from the small metal box and placed the finely ground tobacco behind his lower lip. Once his dip had settled into place he continued to sip the hot coffee from the cup in his left hand . . . and he continued to think.

Now that tracker man was gone and Alvin Harding was on his own. If he was anything more than a greenhorn, he would know that his first act must be to secure provisions. If he knew anything at all of the country in which he now rode, he would make for South Pass. From there they could proceed south along the edge of Antelope Flats, across the Divide and on to Fort Bridger, Utah and to California, if indeed California was his intended destination. But what about Green River? It would be less than a half-day's ride farther and would offer a number of escape routes from which he could choose, but did Harding know of the place? It was certainly something for the old man to consider.

He was thinking of those things when his thoughts returned to his old friend, Antelope Horn. They had been friends for many years. How had they come to be where they were when the old Sioux had been shot down? What events had brought them to Casper and tragedy? He shook his white head and thought to himself, 'Reckon that's what we get fer being Good Samaritans . . . ' Then he gave thought to that day he had first seen the girl.

2

Nine months earlier

With his long-glass the old man had sat at the base of a lodgepole pine that stood tall next to a large limestone boulder. He had watched as the rider steadily drew closer to him. Although that rider had still been nearly two miles away, the old man had been able to see that he was doing everything he could to hide what little trail he was leaving. The old man had been certain that this rider, whoever he was, was being chased.

While he had watched, he had leaned against the pine and chewed on a mouthful of buffalo jerky. 'Just my luck,' he had mumbled to himself, 'to have some pilgrim wander into my camp . . . and a pilgrim trying to outrun trouble at that.'

As he had watched the approaching

rider, from up the hillside behind him the old man had heard the dried pine needles stir and had known that Antelope Horn was making his way down to join him.

Antelope Horn was a Sioux, eight years the old man's junior. He was short and lean in build, but strong and fearless in nature. The old man had found his Sioux friend in the autumn, some nineteen years earlier. The Indian had shot an arrow into an elk, followed the blood trail, found the large antlered beast sprawled on the ground and had presumed him dead. When Antelope Horn had walked up to the downed animal, the bull had risen in one last fit of anger, lowered his massively antlered head and had charged the Sioux brave, pinning him to the ground.

The old man had been watching from higher up on the same mountainside and had seen the Sioux release his arrow. He had followed the elk and its pursuer and had heard the commotion raised when the bull had gored his assailant. He had hurriedly drawn closer to have a better look, only to find the brave lying on the ground, impaled on the elk's antler. He had said, 'Durn fool thing to walk up to an animal without putting another one in him to make sure he's finished. But ... I reckon anybody can make a mistake.' So he had shot the elk with his rifle, just to make sure of him, then he had given aid to the injured brave and nursed him back to health. The two men had been inseparable since.

The old man was thinking about those days and smiling to himself, when Antelope Horn had squatted next to him and said, '*Ishta.*'

'Reckon? A woman? You reckon, Horn?'

'Uh,' the Sioux had grunted, 'a woman ... maybe young woman. You watch. Look see how she sit in saddle.'

The old man had brought his long-glass back to his eye and looked once more. The rider had been closer then, just over a mile away.

'You might be right, Horn. What-in-the-cat-hair's a woman doing a way out here all by her lonesome? Looks to me like she's trying to cover her trail, too, so I reckon she's running from somebody. What ya reckon, Horn?'

'Uh,' the Indian had grunted once more. 'We watch woman's backtrail.'

The old man had nodded in agreement. From their vantage point high on the eastern slope of Big Mountain, they had been watching the rider proceed up the canyon by way of Wolf Creek, in which she now walked her horse. Suddenly the brave had placed his hand on the old man's shoulder and had pointed past the mouth of the canyon to the prairie beyond. 'Them that follow.'

He had been right. There, several miles east and a bit north of the mouth of the canyon had been more riders, although he had not been certain just how many there were; there had been at least five, but he hadn't believed that there had been more than ten. At that distance they had been only a dark speck and a small cloud of dust on the prairie, but they had been there. For a few seconds they had disappeared, dropping into the low ground of a wash or gully, but soon they had reappeared.

Then they had stopped. Probably lost the tracks and trying to cut the woman's trail again, the old man had thought. From what he had seen while watching her ride into the canyon, the old man had been able to tell that she was a smart one and had managed to hide her trail . . . for the moment, anyway.

He and Antelope Horn had lived in these mountains for several years and had only been bothered by outsiders a few times. He had wanted nothing more than to allow these strangers, these interlopers upon his secluded world, to pass by and to have no contact with them. The group would never have known that the two men were even in the neighborhood.

But he had known that neither he nor Antelope Horn could allow a woman in need to pass by without their at least making an attempt to help her. 'Horn, you drop down yonder to where she rode into the creek. Cover her back-trail as best ya can; cover it as far back outside the mouth of the canyon as possible before them rascals get too close. I'll ease over the edge north of here, cut her off then bring her up Alden Creek and over on to Walker Prairie. I'll have her make it appear that she's headed south towards Prairie Creek, then I'll turn her back west towards home. I reckon we can take her to the cabin fer a few days; we can do that much to help her. Depending on how fast she can travel, we ought to be back to the cabin around dark or so — and you watch your topknot.'

Antelope Horn had nodded and, without saying a word, he had eased his way down the mountain toward the mouth of Wolf Creek. The old man had slipped off to the north, making his way down the mountain using all of the cover available to him.

★ ★ ★

Alvin Harding had sat his horse on the open prairie a few miles east of the Big Horns and had watched the others cast about. He had been so angry that he had wrung his hat in his hands. Old Man Buckner's wife had died only a month before and his gold claim on Spearfish Peak had only produced enough color over the preceding months to allow the man to purchase a couple of slabs of side meat, a sack of flour and two sacks of coffee. He was desperate for a grubstake and had nothing of value to sell or trade, so he had thought.

Harding and his friends had been loitering around Saloon No 3 in Lead, when Buckner had entered the establishment in search of a free drink and that grubstake. Harding's cousin, Ben Anderson, had pointed to Buckner and told Alvin of the man's plight and of his sixteen-year-old daughter. Harding had eventually approached Buckner and bought him a drink. He had listened as the man had rambled on about his wife's illness and eventual death, his useless daughter and his need for building materials to work his claim. Finally, after several drinks, they had struck a deal. Buckner had sold his daughter Maggie to Alvin Harding.

When Maggie had been told of the deal, she protested vigorously, but to no avail. Harding had bound her hands and tied her on the back of a horse. They had left Buckner's claim on False Bottom Creek, which was nothing more than a ramshackle cabin and some haphazard diggings, and had ridden west. They had traveled for only a short time before making their camp that first night on Tomcat Creek.

Still with her hands bound, Maggie had sat and watched the eight young men drink themselves into a collective stupor. Twice she had feared that one or more of the men would harm her in some way, but no one had made any attempt to molest her. They had become rowdy, talking loudly among themselves and had argued on more than one occasion, but no one had approached her. Once they had all passed out, Maggie had managed to free her hands of their rawhide bindings, quietly saddled the best horse of the lot and had ridden as hard and as fast as she could, scattering their horses as she had left their camp.

Two days of hard riding, stopping only long enough for her to drink and water her horse, had brought her to the Big Horn Mountains and the mouth of Wolf Creek. Several times she had covered her trail as best she knew how, but had bought for herself only a little added time to make her escape. As she approached Wolf Creek, she knew that Harding and his group could be only a few miles behind.

In his home town Ben Anderson had been considered a good tracker. As a youngster he had roamed the woodlands of Southern Ohio where he had hunted and fished along the banks of the Ohio River. Now at the age of twenty, he was a seasoned hunter and tracker, and had been able to follow the trail left by Maggie Buckner; he had lost the trail more than once, but had found it again each time. Now, following her tracks into a wide gully a few miles east of Big Mountain, he had lost it again.

'I thought you were a tracker, Ben,' Alvin had scorned, as he twisted the hat in his hands. 'It's a wonder you've been able to eat all these years, tracking no better than you do. I find it hard to believe that a clang flip of a girl can throw you off her trail like she has been. She's making a fool of you.'

Ben had become irritated with his cousin's constant mocking. He knew that he could follow a trail and had believed that he would have no problems tracking Maggie Buckner, but the girl had proved to have knowledge more like that of a seasoned hunter rather than that of a sixteen-year-old Illinois farm girl.

When she could, she had ridden in

28

creeks and streams, thus leaving few tracks which he could follow. On more than one occasion it had been completely by accident that he had found signs of her passing, either in the bottom of a stream bed or along its banks. She had traveled across rocky ground when possible and again, it had been by sheer chance that he had found the white streak left by a horseshoe; only by finding one streak here and another there had he been able to stay on her trail. Finally, she had dragged brush behind her horse to distort any tracks that were left on the hard, open ground.

But, regardless of how much pure, dumb luck had played in his being able to trail the girl, he had not allowed his cousin to continue to ridicule him and belittle his skills. 'Alvin, I've put up with your bellyaching long enough. If you think you can do a better job, have at it.'

But Alvin was not a tracker; he was not a woodsman. Alvin Harding was a city boy, having grown up in a small town on the Miami River just a short distance north of Cincinnati. His father had been a shopkeeper and young Alvin had helped him around the store. He knew little or nothing of tracking, so he had been totally dependent upon his cousin to trail the girl, whom he had purchased and had subsequently fled from him.

While Anderson and the others had ridden to and fro searching for a track, he had gradually calmed himself and pulled his hat down on his head. 'I'm sorry, Ben. I'm just mad. I paid good money for that girl and I want her back — I'll have her back!'

After a few minutes of searching, finally Ben had found a track . . . then another. 'She's heading for that gap in the hillside, Alvin. It looks like there might be a creek or something there. Let's ride.'

The eight men had ridden at a ground-covering lope toward the gap in the hillside at which Ben had pointed.

Having decided that Maggie Buckner had most certainly ridden toward the opening in the mountainside, they had abandoned the trail, expecting to pick it up again somewhere in the vicinity of the gap.

* * *

As Harding and his men had ridden toward the place where the rider had entered the water, the old man had traveled around the mountain to intercept her, while Antelope Horn had made his way to the mouth of the canyon. Once there, the old Sioux had quickly brushed away her tracks on the prairie for nearly 200 yards outside the canyon. After brushing away the tracks he had scattered loose dirt over the areas that he had brushed, thus covering most of the brush marks. By the time he had made his way back to the place where the woman had entered the creek, only the most experienced of trackers could have found any sign of her passing, He had returned to the cover of the trees, standing just inside the edge of the timber, and had been looking over his work for only a few minutes when he saw the eight riders approaching.

They had neared the mouth of the canyon and cast about, but they had found nothing. Once again, Alvin had been beside himself with anger. Hidden among the rocks and trees, the old Sioux brave had watched and listened to the tantrum thrown by the irate man on the dark bay gelding. Antelope Horn had chuckled at what he saw and heard.

While the Indian had worked to remove the rider's tracks, the old man had moved quickly but silently, his moccasin-clad feet making only a whisper of a sound as he had made his way across the face of the mountain to intercept the rider. The sun had been nearly overhead and the temperature had risen into the upper sixties. It was late August and the weather had been quite pleasant, but the surrounding peaks of Black, Horseshoe, and Big Mountains were already glistening with snow. Some of the aspen leaves had already begun their metamorphosis to their brilliant yellow and, as he crept around the rocks and over deadfalls, the old man thought that it would be an early winter.

Half an hour after leaving Antelope Horn, the old man had found the rider, who had continued to walk the horse in the water of Wolf Creek. Five minutes later, he had made his presence known.

'Ease up yonder, missy,' the old man had said softly.

Startled, she had pulled on the reins sharply, jerking her mount to a halt. 'Who are you, mister, and what do you want?'

The old man had smiled. She was just a girl, maybe sixteen or so, and pretty as a patch of blue columbine at the edge of an aspen grove. She had been dressed in an old gray flannel shirt and black canvas breeches. She was wearing a pair of worn out flat-heeled boots and had a battered, flat-crowned gray hat pulled down over a shock of auburn hair. She had sported no sidearm, but there had been a Henry rifle in the scabbard that was tied to the offside of the saddle.

'Easy does her, young lady. I ain't here to harm ya,' the old man had said in a soft, quieting tone. 'Me and my partner's been up yonder on this here mountain watching ya fer some time . . . you making your way off'n the prairie and up Wolf Creek, here. It appeared to us that ya's trying to cover your trail . . . then we seen them others coming, back out a ways on the flat land. We reckoned ya might be in need of some help.'

She had quickly surveyed the area around her, hoping to find the partner as this stranger had called him, but could find no one else. Then she had looked back at the old man and repeated, 'Who are you, mister?'

The old man chuckled and continued

to smile. 'Zimmerman, ma'am. Ezekiel Zimmerman. Them that knows me calls me Zeke . . . and other things. That other feller what I referred to is my ole friend, Antelope Horn. Me and Horn live in this neck of the woods. Like I said, we was over south and east of here and seen ya come in off the prairie. Watched ya riding easy like up the creek here and decided that if ya needed our help, we'd offer it. Ole Horn's already gone out yonder to cover your back-trail. If ya want my help, just foller me.'

Without another word the old man had turned and walked up the creek, still in the water so as to make no tracks on the muddy banks; he had not looked back to see if the girl was following.

For half a mile the old man had walked at a steady pace. He could hear the gentle splashes of the horse's hoofs in the water behind him. Suddenly he had turned sharply south, made his way up a dry, rocky streambed to its head, then over a low saddle and down the other side, using a similar streambed as before.

Within a few minutes they were standing at the western base of Big Mountain and at the eastern edge of what was known as Walker Prairie, a long grassy valley that lay north-west to south-east for some twelve miles. It began just north of where they now stood and narrowed to an end at Big Goose Creek, just south of She-Bear Mountain.

There they had separated for a time, giving the impression — should his tracks be found — that they had been made at a different time, hopefully convincing those who followed that the girl was still alone. He had instructed her to keep the same pace and ride along the edge of the timber for a few hundred yards. Then she was to turn due west and cross the half-mile of open ground to a lone aspen tree, toward which he pointed, at the mouth of Gloom Creek. There he would be waiting for her.

With his Henry laid over his shoulder, the old man had walked due south, crossing the grassy valley at an angle, always careful to leave as little sign as possible. When the girl had walked her horse up to the mouth of Gloom Creek, the old man had already been moving upstream, staying to the cold clear water of the creek.

He had lived in these mountains for many years, dodging hostile Indians and others. He could follow the faintest of trails and could hide one better than anyone he knew, with the exception of perhaps Antelope Horn. Few people even knew of his existence and most of those had no idea he lived in these mountains or how to find him.

To be honest, the old man didn't like most people. They were always in a hurry and money, or what it could buy, was the most important thing in the world to most of them. On the other hand, he seldom got into any sort of a hurry and money, although he had all he ever needed, was the least of his concerns. He cared more to sit by the fire with a good pinch of snuff and a hot cup of coffee than for all of the big houses, fancy clothes or any other foolishness that folks in civilization worried over.

Along an old, much used game trail, the old man had steadily moved up and around the face of the mountain to the small spring where Wolf Creek was born; he had traveled in a wide semi-circle and had covered nearly nine miles. Then, leaving the game trail, he had turned west again, crossing over the top of the ridge. Once more he had turned at right angles, located another game trail and followed it north along the backside of the mountain. The sun had nearly disappeared behind the peaks of Black Mountain and the shadows in the timber had become quite dark when, having used every device available to him, he had finally made his way along the eastern edge of a lush valley to the middle of the mile-long meadow east of Black Mountain where his cabin stood.

It was a large, well-constructed log edifice, some thirty feet square, built well back from the edge of the meadow in a deep hollow at the base of a sheer rock wall; the overhang protruded nearly ten feet out over the front edge of the house. There was a stone fireplace on both the east and west ends of the building, with a heavily shuttered window near the front corner of each end, as well as a large window on either side of the front door. It was built of ten-inch hewed logs with a flat roof that sloped from front to back. It was a likely house built in a likely spot.

Firewood sufficient to see its occupants through the coldest of winters had been neatly stacked outside against the front of the house. A large meathouse stood near its west end; the girl had no doubt that it was filled with elk, deer and/or buffalo meat. On the east end of the house was a corral that was attached to the front of a barn; there was a hollowed stone trough of water in one corner of the corral. Hay had been stacked in a huge pile inside a second pole corral next to the barn. Once the old man had turned the girl's bay into the first corral with his animals, he had led the way into the house.

He had shown her inside and then began the process of rekindling the fire, as Maggie surveyed her accommodations. Near the back wall on each end of the house were two beds ... not bunks, but heavy, four-post bed frames with ropes woven from side to side and top to bottom. Elk skins had been stitched together and stuffed with pine-straw, then laid atop the ropes to make each a soft, comfortable bed.

The fireplaces were beautifully constructed of flat rocks that had been carefully fitted and placed, leaving an opening that would accommodate a three-foot log. There were a pair of cooking cranes in the fireplace on the east end of the house, one of which held a large pot, which the old man had swung into place once the fire had been coaxed back to life.

In the front corner near that same fireplace were a table and two chairs. In the center of the table there sat a half-filled crock of honey and a tin plate that held a large loaf of fresh bread. In that same corner, there were shelves along the wall upon which had been placed canned goods, containers of sugar, coffee and at least a dozen boxes of cartridges. Along the remaining walls there sat stacks of skins, which had been tied into bales. She recognized skunk, marmot and badger skins as well as those of wolves, cougars and bobcats. Along the back wall were bales of deer, elk and moose hides and one large bale of buffalo hides. She had estimated that the collection of prime skins would amount to a small fortune.

Her survey of the cabin was suddenly cut short by the old man. 'Come over and have yourself a chair at the table, girlie. Supper'll be ready as soon as the stew heats back up.'

She had walked to the table, taken a

seat and watched as the old man dipped water into a coffee pot. Then he had scooped a handful of dark, ground coffee from an Arbuckle's bag, dumped it into the water and had then set the pot on a large flat rock at the edge of the fire. The cabin had begun to smell delightfully like — home.

As the sun had disappeared behind the mountains, the evening air had grown chilled, but with the fire blazing in the fireplace the cabin had grown warmer and the girl had begun to feel the effects of her travels. Her eyelids grew heavy and she had laid her head down upon her folded arms, which rested on the table.

'I'll rest for just a few minutes,' she had said, thinking aloud, but her words faded as she had relaxed and drifted off to sleep.

3

Maggie had sat at the table for several minutes, asleep with her head on her arms. The old man had already placed bowls, cups and spoons on the table. When the door opened and Antelope Horn had stepped inside, she awoke with a start, sitting bolt upright in her chair.

'Easy, girlie,' the old man had said to calm her, 'you're amongst friends. You dropped off to sleep. Have yourself a bowl of stew, then you can get yourself a good long nap.'

He had ladled stew from the pot into the bowls as the Sioux hung his rifle on two pegs that were driven into holes that had been drilled in the wall, and his possible bag over another; several other long guns and the old man's possible bag hung in the same fashion. By the time Antelope Horn had been seated, the old man had cut thick slices of bread off of the loaf.

As Maggie awoke fully, the fogginess left her head she remembered where she was and the circumstances that had brought her there. She had looked first at the Indian who sat near her at the table. He had said nothing, but smiled and nodded to her. Then she had taken a critical look at the old man, not at all certain that she was liking what she saw.

He was not a big man, maybe five feet nine inches in height and 150 pounds or so. The top of his head was completely bald and, like his wrinkled face and hands, baked dark by many hours in the sun. But on the rest of his head and face, his hair and beard were snow white, his heavy beard long and untrimmed and his thick mane hung to his shoulders.

She guessed his age to be in his late-fifties and probably eight to ten years older than his Sioux companion. His shoulders sloped slightly, and she had thought she had detected a slight limp as he walked.

Both men were clad in homemade buckskins, probably made from hides from the animals they themselves had trapped, and each man had carried a converted Navy Colt pistol, along with a long-bladed, bone-handled knife and a Henry rifle.

'Where ya heading, girlie?' the old man had asked.

He hadn't asked about her troubles, although he had already guessed that she had them. She had suddenly somehow realized that he would not pry; he would not ask too many questions of her for fear she might not wish to answer. They had helped her by removing her tracks and had given her refuge. That night she would not be hungry and she would have a warm place to sleep. At that moment, she had been certain that she would be safe there with these men for as long as she needed, or chose, to stay with them.

'I have relatives in Oregon. I suppose I'll head west and try to find them.'

The old man had nodded. 'That's a far piece, girlie, to be traveling alone.' He spooned up another bite of the stew, then added, 'I'd figure the stage would be the safest way fer a young girl to make that trip. You could catch yourself a coach down to Old Fort Casper.'

The stage . . . she had not given it any thought. She hadn't had time to give thought to anything more than just being away from Alvin Harding and his friends. She had known that her aunt's family had a farm somewhere in southern Oregon near a small town called Ashland; her uncle David had moved their family West in 1869. Maggie had been very close to her aunt Jessie, her mother's sister, and Uncle David while growing up near Mt Vernon, Illinois, and had been sad to see them leave. She had received at least one letter each year since they had settled in Oregon and in each letter Jessie had encouraged Maggie's father to join them there. The land there was fertile and her uncle was knowledgeable and hard-working, so they had prospered immensely. Her aunt had written in one of her last letters that their small farm had grown to nearly double its original acreage.

She would travel to Oregon and join her aunt's family there. But she had no money with which to purchase passage on the stagecoach, to buy her meals, nor to purchase proper clothing. She would first have to earn enough money to make such a trip, which meant that she must go to a town and live there for as long as it took. Or, she had thought, she could continue on horseback, alone. After all, she had a rifle with which she could supply her own meat. She could purchase neither flour nor coffee, but she could drink water and she could do without biscuits and hoecakes.

'Well,' she said, after hesitating to gather her thoughts, 'I'm not certain what to do exactly. I left in such a hurry. The only thing I was thinking about was how to get away from those men.'

The old man nodded again, but said nothing. When she had first met him, she had feared that she might be 'jumping out of the frying pan and into the fire', but she no longer had those fears. He had been calm, sure of himself and polite when first they had met, not insisting that she follow him, but offering to help her if she would accept his assistance. Sitting there at their table she had been certain that these men had simply befriended a young woman in need and she became more and more comfortable. She also believed that if she asked his advice, the old man would give it. She had been equally as certain that, inside the mind of this old man, there was great wisdom into which she could tap.

'If I may offer just one piece of advice,' the old man had interjected, 'the first thing that ya need to think about is giving them fellers enough time to get outta this part of the country. As long as they're in the neighborhood, it won't be safe fer you to travel. If I was you, I'd stay put fer a few days, give them fellers a chance to decide to look fer ya down to the south and let them move on. While you're waiting, you can mull over your options and figure out what you're gonna do. Me and ole Horn have got to travel down to Casper in a couple of weeks anyhow; you're welcome to ride along with us.'

She hadn't asked for his advice, but he had offered words of wisdom, which she would certainly heed. 'Thank you, Mister . . . I'm sorry, I don't remember your name. I'm Margaret Buckner — everyone calls me Maggie.'

'Zimmerman, ma'am, Ezekiel Zimmerman.' The old man had smiled again and said. 'You can call me Zeke, ma'am. This here's Antelope Horn. Horn here's a Sioux. Me and him have been friends fer twenty years, give or take.'

Maggie had smiled back. 'Thank you, Mr Zimmerman . . . Zeke. I would hate to impose upon you, but I am desperate

49

to stay out of the hands of those men.'

'No imposition at all, girlie. You're welcome here.'

He had not probed into her circumstances, but she realized that, if she was to ask his advice, she must first give him all of the facts with which to deal.

'Mr Zimmerman, my father sold our farm in Illinois and moved us out here to Spearfish Peak; we arrived last November. Mother fell ill during our trip and became totally dependent upon me, not long after Daddy staked his claim on False Bottom Creek.

'He had the gold fever and I suppose he was providing for us as best he could, but his claim showed little color. Because we've had so little snow and rain this year, by mid July the creek hadn't much water flowing in it. Daddy kept insisting that he needed more water to work his diggings, so he had to have money to build a flume, sluice, rocker box or whatever you call it. We were on light rations and stayed hungry most of the time; Momma became weaker with every new day. Daddy began drinking heavily and was spending as much time at the saloons in Lead as he spent working his claim. Then he started hitting Momma and me when he came home. He'd be drunk and that always meant that he was in a bad mood and quarrelsome; he'd start an argument over nothing at all. He kept saying that if he hadn't the extra mouths to feed, he would have more money to use for the things he needed to work the claim and for his own supplies.

'I woke one morning back three weeks ago and made coffee and biscuits for Daddy's breakfast. Momma was still in bed; I knew she wasn't well, so I let her sleep. I saw him off to his diggings and went about my chores. It grew late in the morning, but Momma hadn't stirred. When I checked on her, I found that she was dead — died in her sleep I suppose.

'Momma and Daddy had always been very happy when we lived in

Illinois.' Tears ran down her cheeks as she had choked out the words. 'Daddy was a good farmer and we had a nice place back there. We had a nice home . . . not a big fancy house, but it was a good home, warm and comfortable. And we always had plenty to eat. Daddy raised large crops of corn and wheat, and we had a few cows, both for meat and for milking. We had family who lived close by and friends who always helped us with the harvest each year, so he was never out any wages and made a good return for his labors.

'Momma and I raised a garden every year. We grew all of the things one usually finds in a vegetable garden, and we dried or canned enough vegetables to last us the entire year and then some. She and I picked apples from our own trees and made jelly, and we gathered blackberries and strawberries and made preserves. It was a good life and an excellent living. Momma was flabbergasted when Daddy informed her that he had sold the farm and was moving us to the goldfields of South Dakota. I honestly believe that it broke her heart and once she became ill, I think she just gave up.

'A few days ago — I'm not even certain how many days it's been — Daddy came home from the saloons, drunk as usual. He walked in with a young man he called Alvin Harding and informed me that I was to go with this Harding and not to give him any trouble. When I refused to leave, Harding bound my hands and tied me on a horse. Daddy didn't even say goodbye.'

She was sobbing by the time she'd finished her story, so the old man had patted her on the shoulder in an attempt to console her. Suddenly, she had blurted in anger, 'Those men told me that my daddy *sold* me! You want to know what he thought I was worth? I'll tell you what I was worth to him . . . an old sway-back nag of a horse, a worn-out old buffalo coat and sixty dollars in gold.'

The old man and the Sioux had looked at each other across the table. Antelope Horn had nodded, and the old man had known exactly what it had meant.

'Well, Miss Maggie, ole Horn there shot hisself a bull elk a few years back; stuck him with a arrow right behind his shoulder . . . and it were a mighty good shot, too. He follered the blood and found him lying all sprawled out on the ground. 'Course, he figured the elk to be dead. Now ole Horn was a much younger man in them days, and he weren't quite as knowing as he is now, so, he walks right up on that ole bull without making sure of him.'

The old man had continued telling the story of his finding the injured Sioux brave and of their ensuing friendship. Then he had added, 'So ya see, Miss Maggie, anybody can make a mistake and most ever'body I know has at one time or the other. Horn here didn't make sure his elk was dead before walking up on him . . . got him hurt. Your dad caught the gold fever and it's been the downfall of many a good man. Somebody mentions gold, and something inside of some folks' head goes haywire. They stop thinking straight; start treating them that's closest to them like they's dirt under their feet — or worse than dirt. He surely done a bad thing, Miss Maggie, but I heared a Methodist preacher one time say that the Good Lord would fergive us fer all the wrongs we've done ag'in him and other folks. That same preacher also said that the Good Lord expected us to fergive them that does wrong ag'in us. Seems to me a body'd sleep better at night if they could see things the way that preacher did, but I reckon it's a thing that's easier said than done though.'

They had remained quiet then, while they had eaten the stew. Eventually they finished their supper and Antelope Horn had poured hot water into a dishpan and was washing their bowls. Then the old man motioned to the girl to follow him. 'Let's you and me fix you up a comfortable bed, Miss Maggie.'

So he and Maggie arranged a few of the fur bales in the front corner opposite the table. After dragging the bales together, the old man had laid half-dozen elk hides over them, then three heavy blankets over the hides, then folded a third and placed it on one end for her to use as a pillow. In just a few minutes, her bed had been made and ready for her use. The girl had bade the two old men good-night, then she had pulled off her boots and crawled into her bed. She had snuggled deep into her blankets as she had watched the old man walk to the rear of the house. From one of the stacks on a table beside his bed he had lifted a book and a pair of spectacles, then he walked back to the table. In the light of the oil lamp that sat in its center, he opened the book, removed his marker and, with the aid of his specs, became engrossed in its text as he followed each line with his finger. She had not remembered closing her eyes. She had only remembered thinking that during that night she would be warm and comfortable . . . and safe.

4

While the old man had guided the girl toward the cabin, Harding's group searched for any sign of her trail. For the rest of the afternoon, Ben Anderson scoured the ground outside the mouth of the canyon through which Wolf Creek flowed, while the others searched farther out on the prairie. Twice, one of the others had called to him, thinking that they had found a sign of Maggie's passing, but neither had proved to be her track. He had become frustrated at his inability to track the girl. She was only sixteen years of age and certainly could not be so experienced in the woods as to be able to elude him with such expertise. He had eventually ridden back to the bank of the draw where he had last seen her tracks. Methodically he had followed the trail until it petered out and disappeared again a couple of hundred yards before it reached the canyon.

That night the group had made their camp along the banks of Wolf Creek, not ten yards from where the girl had entered the water. While their supper had been prepared, the members of the group had voiced their opinions regarding the girl and Alvin Harding had devised a plan.

'Harding, we should just forget about that dang girl,' Tom Ferguson fervently argued. 'We stole that old nag and the coat was worn out, and sixty bucks ain't worth all this confounded trouble.'

'Yeah, Alvin, I've got to agree with Tommy,' Kevin Love had contended. 'We need to be moving on. I've heard that the weather could get bad around here at any time. We need to get on across the Divide if we're gonna make it to California before winter sets in.'

Alvin looked across the fire at his brother, Arnold, who had been staring back at him and nodding in agreement with the others. It galled the man that he had lost the girl, but it had become more apparent, with every hour that passed, that they would not locate any sign of her passing, making it highly unlikely that they would ever find her.

Harding had been angry and reluctant to give up completely. '*All right!* But she could have doubled back and headed to a town near here, so, in the morning, Ben, you take Arnold, Sam, Jim and Charlie and head for Buffalo — you said it's a couple of hours or so ride south-east of here. I'll take Tommy and Kevin with me and ride north to Sheridan. Check any camp, cabin, barn, house, outhouse and henhouse you come across between here and there. Ask everyone you see about anybody in these parts that she could have met up with. If I haven't found her by the time we reach Sheridan, and if she ain't there, we'll forget about her. If you find her, leave Arnold in Buffalo to wait for us; you hold on to the girl and the rest of you make a camp outside of town. Find her or not, Tommy, Kevin and I will head for Buffalo from Sheridan and meet you there . . . then we'll move on.'

The following morning, the group had split into two parties and headed in different directions. Unbeknownst to the eight riders, the girl had spent the night having eaten a good meal and had slept warm and comfortable in a bed comprised of prime furs.

* * *

After a good night's sleep, Maggie awakened to the smell and sound of bacon frying. When she opened her eyes, she had seen the old man bending over a huge cast-iron skillet, which sat on an iron grate just inside the edge of the fireplace. She had inhaled deeply, taking in the mouthwatering aromas of the cured side-meat and the coffee, which had already begun to boil.

The old man was forking the well-done strips of meat into a pile on a tin plate when she swung her legs over the edge of her makeshift bed. He had

61

placed the plateful of bacon on the table, along with three empty cups and plates, then he had turned back to his skillet and made gravy. When the gravy was ready, he had placed the large skillet in the center of the table and then walked toward the door.

As he had made his way to the open door to call out for Antelope Horn, he looked in the girl's direction and saw that she was already awake. 'Come and get it, missy, before I throw it out to the chickens.' His cheeks had wrinkled as he formed a smile that had barely shown through his long, curved, white mustache.

She had returned the smile. 'It certainly smells good, Mr Zimmerman.' Embarrassed, she added, 'I can't remember the last time I slept while breakfast was being prepared.'

The old man stepped through the door and called for Antelope Horn. When he walked back through the door, he was still smiling. 'Well, Miss Maggie, other than a couple of our friends from down south of here, you're the first visitor we've had in nigh on fifteen years. Now reckon how it would look fer us to be having our guests roll outta bed and fix their own vittles? Why, word might get around and we'd never have no more company.'

The girl had laughed out loud. 'Well, I promise, if anyone asks me, I'll make certain that they know that you treat your guests like royalty. Really! How many people do you know that sleep in a fur bed?' With the smile still barely showing under its hairy white cover, he nodded and gave her a wave to come to the table.

The sky had turned gray when the old Sioux brave returned from his morning chores carrying a dutch oven, which he had placed on the table next to the skillet of gravy. They had taken their seats, the old man seated on a small bale of furs, and each had eaten a large portion of bacon, biscuits and gravy, along with several cups of the coffee. Maggie's mother would have said that she 'ate like a field hand', and although Maggie had been embarrassed to admit it, she would have been right.

'Missy, there's a fine big waterfall and pool, a couple hundred feet or so out yonder to the west, where you can take yourself a bath. Just walk around the end of the cabin and foller the rock wall into the timber . . . you can't miss it. After you fell asleep last night, Horn there cut-down a set of his buckskins. I reckon they'll fit you good enough so you can wash the clothes you have on.

'Now I try to get out yonder ever' week or so to scrub off the grime. I never could abide being dirty . . . reckon 'cause of my up-bringing. My ma always said, 'folks can be as poor as a whippoorwill, but soap is cheap enough to make and water's free, so there ain't no reason to be dirty'. Now ole Horn here takes three baths a year, whether he needs them or not . . . one in the spring, another 'bout mid-summer and then again in the fall before the weather turns cold. I reckon it'd pay to stay up-wind of him most of the time . . . if you get my meaning.' He was chuckling when he had said it; the old Sioux simply smiled and grunted.

'Thank you, Mr Zimmerman . . . Antelope Horn.' She had wanted to say more, but, even though she had been smiling, the lump in her throat had not allowed it.

She had felt quite filthy; she knew that her face was dirty and that her hair was grimy and matted. She was unable to remember the last time that she had gone so long without bathing. As soon as she had finished her breakfast, the old man handed her a bar of store-bought soap and the buckskins of which he had spoken, then she had walked to the waterfall to bathe.

Even before she reached the edge of the timber, she had heard the sound of the water cascading into the pool. It came from a spring that flowed from the sheer wall of the mountain and cascaded some seventy or eighty feet into the pool that measured nearly twenty feet wide and forty feet long. The water, although quite cold, had been very refreshing; she spent several minutes washing her hair under the waterfall and swimming around the pool, rinsing the soap from her body. Once she had bathed, she had used the bar of soap to scrub her dirty clothes on a rock at the edge of the pool. When her clothes were washed, she pulled on the buckskins, laced up the front of the shirt and tightened the draw string of the breeches around her waist. Remarkably, they had fitted quite well, as though they had been tailored, and she felt human once again.

When she returned to the cabin, she had hung her wet clothes across the top rail of the fence that surrounded the haystack. The old man had already opened a door on the side of the barn nearest the house, releasing more than a dozen Leghorn hens and two roosters, and had been spreading a few handfuls of corn over the area.

'Chickens?' she had asked.

Once again the old man smiled. 'Yes'm. We might live out here in the middle of nowhere, but I like my eggs. And me having growed up in Tennessee, I get a hankering now'n ag'in fer the occasional meal of fried chicken, or chicken and dumplings. Besides, reckon how we've come to have all of them cat and fox pelts baled up inside yonder? We keep traps set around the place, so when them varmints come a'calling fer a chicken dinner, we collect their hides.'

The girl had laughed aloud once again, at this pleasant old man's sense of humor. She could never have imagined that someone could live so well in such a remote location. Once he had finished his chores, the old man gave her the grand tour of their domain.

The shallow brook that flowed from the pool at the base of the waterfall became a narrow, but deep, stream that flowed across the meadow several yards north-west of the cabin. The two men had dug canals that connected to the stream, allowing them to irrigate a sizeable garden. There had been a crop of corn and beans, all of which had been picked and dried. She had observed hills of potatoes, several large cabbages, a couple of bushels of carrots and several gigantic cushaws. It had appeared to her that nearly all of the remaining vegetables were ready to be harvested, with the exception of a few of the cushaws. She had seen the effects of wildlife having taken a share of their yield, but there would be more than enough to feed the two men until their next crop was raised.

'I'm very impressed, Mr Zimmerman.' Her father had been a very good farmer, there in Illinois, but she doubted that he could have done as well as these men had, here in these mountains.

'Well, we started out by growing the vegetables the Indians in these parts grow and saved our own seeds. Then every spring we clean out the barn and chicken house and use the manure fer fertilizer. Since we dug them canals, the garden gets plenty of water all summer long, so them vegetables grow fast and there's always been enough to get us through.

'There's a shaller cave in behind the cabin that we use fer our root cellar; we laid stones and built a wall across the opening to keep the varmints out. The temperature inside stays near the same year round, so the potaters, carrots and kraut keep mighty well in yonder. I've got myself a dozen crocks in the barn, and I chop up and pickle the cabbage in them and make my sauerkraut. We make up sausages from some of the elk and moose we kill, so we slice up some of that sausage into the kraut, cook it down, then bake us some cornbread . . . makes fer a mighty good feed. I reckon we've got 'bout everything we need and that's all a body can ask fer.'

As they had walked back toward the cabin, she admitted, 'I would never have guessed someone could be so self-sufficient, here in such a wilderness.' He only chuckled at her remark.

The old man had suggested that she relax for a couple of days, so she had spent the remainder of that day lounging around the cabin. The door and the window shutters had been left open, so there had been lots of fresh air and the cabin had smelled of the mountain pines. Since the inside of the cabin had been adequately lit by the light from outside, after having asked the old man to borrow any book that he thought she would enjoy, she had lain on her bed and had begun to read Daniel Defoe's *The Life and Strange Surprising Adventures of Robinson Crusoe*. It was early afternoon and the sun had shone on the front of the buildings, making the cabin comfortably warm. Before she could finish the first page, she had fallen asleep.

When she had again left her bed and walked outside the cabin, the sun was only an orange fireball perched atop the peaks of Black Mountain. She could not believe that she had fallen asleep at all, let alone had slept for such a long time.

The old man and Antelope Horn had been working in their garden. As she had stepped through the door, they were returning to the cabin leading two horses which pulled sleds loaded with vegetables; she remembered having thought earlier that they appeared ready to be harvested.

'Have yourself a good nap, missy?'

She had smiled and stretched. 'Yes, thank you. I'm surprised that I fell asleep, but it looks like the two of you have been busy while I napped.'

He had nodded and said that they had been planning for several days to make his sauerkraut, so they had decided to start right away. He had told her that he had a feeling that the weather would turn cold soon and that he was concerned about losing the remainder of their vegetable crop. He would now make his sauerkraut while Antelope Horn dug their potatoes. When that was finished, they would pull what remained of their carrot crop, but they would leave the corn on the stalks until it was dried and ready to be ground into meal, as well as feed for the chickens.

After unloading the heads of cabbage at the cabin, Antelope Horn had led the second horse to the rear of the building and stored the remaining vegetables in the cave. While he was gone, the girl had talked with the old man.

'Mr Zimmerman, may I ask your advice about something?'

As the old man chopped at a large head of cabbage with a long, thick-bladed knife, he had once again smiled through his long white mustache and nodded. Although he had made it his policy to ride shy of other folk's business, he had expected, or maybe only hoped, that she would seek guidance regarding her journey to Oregon, 'I reckon so, missy. What's on your mind?'

'Well, I'm going to need money, so I'll have to go to some town and work until I can earn enough to get me to my aunt and uncle's farm in Oregon. How close is the nearest town . . . where I could find work, I mean?'

The old man had chuckled and continued to smile. 'Well, missy, me and Ole Horn was talking about that very thing, while we was down yonder in the garden.' He stopped speaking long enough to place another cabbage on the table and had then continued to hack away. 'Well, like I's saying, me and Horn was talking on the subject of your traveling to Oregon, and he figured we oughta purchase ya a ticket on the stage, and see to it ya had the clothes and whatever else a young lady needs to make such a journey. And he figures we oughta make sure ya have enough cash money to see ya through fer a while . . . 'til ya can get settled.'

She had tears in her eyes, but she was shaking her head while he spoke. 'Mr Zimmerman, I appreciate your generosity. It will take me some time to earn it, but I prefer to get the money that way.'

He had chuckled, again, at her

answer, because he had told the old Sioux that they should expect just such a response. She was obviously a proud girl with wisdom beyond her years, but, when trading furs for what they needed, he could be quite the haggler, so with that wide smile still on his face, he had begun his haggling. 'Now, missy, we ain't got nobody in this ole world . . . me nor him . . . and when we go under, this here place'll probably go back to nature. She'll get all growed over ag'in, just like she was before we cleared the timber and built this here cabin. The animals'll turn wild, or get ate by the varmints, and them canals down yonder in that meadow will all fill in — a hundred years from now, a body'd never know we was ever here.

'Over the years, we've saved us up a store of hides and furs, so we trade and sell what we need to, for the buying of what food stores we need. As you see, we don't need much, other than coffee, flour and sugar, besides what we grow ourselves, but there has been times

74

when we wanted some jelly or hard candy, or some such extravagance, so we sell some of our goods fer cash money and just buy whatever it be we's a wanting.

'Now, missy, I realize you don't know us, but we've took a liking to ya already. Ole Horn had a family once, back yonder in '53, a year or so before I found him. Had hisself a young wife and a little boy that he just thought the world and all of. Then in '54 his people was down yonder around Fort Laramie, waiting fer their allotment of food stores the gover'ment had promised in the Treaty of '51. It so happened that them groceries was late getting to the fort, so them Sioux was running low on grub and hungry. As fortune, or misfortune in this case, would have it, 'bout that time a group of Mormons was passing through on their trek to Utah. One of their half-starved ole milk cows wandered off away from their wagons and come a strolling over into that Sioux camp. Indians being Indians and having their own ways of thinking, they figured the cow to be abandoned and a stray, so they butchered and ate the critter.

'Well, to make a long story short, them Mormons claimed the cow was stole, the army got involved, and the whole blamed mess turned into a shooting fracas. When the shooting was over, an entire company of soldiers was wiped out and Antelope Horn's woman and little boy was dead, along with a considerable number of the tribe members, including ole Chief Conquering Bear.

'I'm telling ya all of this so ya know just how much we want to do this fer ya . . . and I reckon we won't take no fer an answer.' Then he had winked at the teary-eyed girl and had added, 'You just think on it fer a spell.'

She wiped away the tears as she strolled outside and seated herself on a bench near the door. The sun had gone down behind Black Mountain, causing its peaks to be crowned by a glorious halo of amber and gold light. Darkness will soon be upon this quiet place, she had thought. It would soon be supper time . . . and suddenly she decided that she would cook for these men.

She had quickly risen and stepped back through the door and asked the old man what he had planned for supper. He had already been layering the cabbage and salt, pressing it into the bottom of one of the large crocks, so he had looked up from his pile of chopped cabbage leaves, surprised and a bit puzzled by the question.

'What I mean is,' she had stammered, 'I want to help out around here, so, if you'll tell me what to cook, I'd like to prepare our supper.'

The old man had nodded and grinned, causing the corners of his white mustache to move upwards, and had told her where she could find her ingredients. Then he had gone back to work preparing his beloved sauerkraut.

5

Over the next few days the girl had rested, but had helped with some of the chores as well. She had swept and dusted the house, watched the old man chop and layer the cabbage and salt in the crocks and had cooked their meals. She had even helped Antelope Horn with the digging and storing of the potatoes. Helping out around the place had been more restful to her than just lying around, for it had given her a good feeling inside . . . like she had felt while working on her family's Illinois farm.

For nearly three weeks she had stayed with the old man and the Sioux. During those weeks they had not mentioned the subject of the girl's monetary needs, but had stayed busy working around the place. By the end of that time, the crops had been harvested and the old man had loaded packs for the trip to Casper.

The temperature had been quite cool as the sky turned gray on the morning of the twentieth day after the girl had come to stay with the two men; the feel of autumn was in the air. Antelope Horn had saddled their horses while the old man had loaded the packs on a mouse-colored dun that he called Gretchen. Then he had opened the door of the chicken house while Antelope Horn had removed the three rails which served as a gate for the corral, led their horses out and had then replaced only the bottom two rails, leaving the top rail off.

'Won't all your animals run off if you leave the door and gate open like that?'

The old man shook his head. 'Well, the chickens don't go far and they'll roost in the trees 'til we get back. They'll come to me when the corn is spread here in the yard. Besides, we couldn't just leave them inside. If we was long in getting back, they might starve. The horses probably won't try to leave the corral as long as they've got hay to eat, so them two bottom rails'll keep them inside, unless they really want ta get out. If we ain't back b'fore the hay runs out, or a big cat or bear comes 'round calling, they can clear them two rails and get outta harm's way. They'll stay here in the valley, so I can beat on a bucket of grain and call fer them and they'll come to me.' He had then gone on about the business of preparing to travel but had added with a chuckle, 'They know which side their bread's buttered on. We've left them like this many a time and besides, me and ole Horn oughta be back here in six days or so.'

She had smiled and nodded, realizing that these men had obviously done this many times over the years. Hadn't the old man told her that they occasionally took some of their furs to one town or another where they traded for the supplies that they need? She had been embarrassed for having asked such a silly question and the old man had seen her embarrassment.

'You know, missy, you're a right smart gal. Most folks fail to ask questions about matters that they don't know the answer to, or don't understand. A body'll never learn nothing if they don't ask questions once in a while . . . no matter how foolish the question might seem at the time.'

She had continued smiling, but it was because she liked this old man; he was thoughtful and kind. She had been embarrassed and he had known it and offered words of encouragement to make her feel better. She would miss him.

As the glowing rim of the sun had risen from the floor of the open prairie and had shone itself over the peaks of Big Mountain, they had ridden away from the cabin *en route* to Fort Casper. The fort itself had been torn down board by board in 1869, and the materials had been moved fifty miles or so down the North Platte River to a plateau near the mouth of La Prele Creek. There the army had used the materials from Fort Casper to build a new fort, Fort Fetterman.

Although the fort was no longer there, the tiny settlement at Platte Bridge Station, or Casper as it had come to be called, had continued to grow slowly. Travelers along the Oregon and Mormon Trails had used the ferry there for many years, until Louis Guinard had built his bridge in 1859. Most of the immigrants had moved on along the trail, toward their dreams in California, Utah or Oregon, but occasionally a family of the travelers had stayed even after the fort had been moved. Thus the small settlement in the Territory of Wyoming, now known as Casper, had grown.

The trio had ridden all day, following game trails when available and had crossed mountain meadows, most of which had still been belly deep in grass. Since they had used switch-back trails up one mountainside and down the other, and because the sun sets early in the mountains making the days short, they had traveled less than thirty miles that first day and had decided to spend that first night on the banks of Emerald Lake.

After the horses had been seen to, the old man had built their fire and put the coffee on, while Antelope Horn had made his way to the rocky bank of the lake to catch their supper. While the old man had worked putting the camp together, the girl had mixed batter for cornbread and soon had the small Dutch oven covered with glowing red coals from the fire. In just a short time Antelope Horn had returned with seven brook trout for the feast and, although the night had the chilled feeling of the approaching winter, the atmosphere in their first night's camp had been most cheerful.

With the trails being smoother and having fewer switch-backs to maneuver, they had made better time over the next two days, so before noon on the fourth day they had crossed the toll bridge at Casper.

6

Once across the bridge, they had stopped in the shade of a lone pine tree that grew on the south bank of the North Platte and had immediately seen to the horses. Once they had been picketed, Antelope Horn and the girl had gathered firewood and put the camp together; the old man disappeared.

Half an hour after beginning their task of setting up the camp, Antelope Horn had the fire going and the girl had placed the coffee pot at its edge, when the old man had casually strolled back into camp giving no explanation as to his absence.

They had passed the remainder of that day by the old man and Antelope Horn showing the girl around the small town, while they had purchased the few supplies which they had needed. She had been shown the stage station, livery, trading post and the few stores and shops, a couple of which had sprung up only a couple of months earlier. Before they had finished their short tour, the old man had disappeared once more.

Antelope Horn and Maggie had returned to their camp. The girl, always being ready to share in the chores, had immediately assembled the ingredients for a batch of biscuits. She had been placing the balls of dough in the Dutch oven when the old man had once again sauntered back into camp. Under his left arm he had carried two packages.

The coffee had already begun to boil and the camp had been filled with that unique fragrance of wood smoke, coffee and baking biscuits, when the old man had handed the girl the packages. 'Me and ole Horn figured you could use these.'

She had taken the packages, looked at them for a few seconds, then had looked back at the old man, who had added sternly, 'It ain't no charity, girlie. They're a gift . . . and folks got a right to give a gift to a friend.'

She had smiled as tears filled her eyes. 'Thank you. Thank you both very much.' She had opened the first, and larger, of the two packages and found a dark-blue linsey-woolsey dress that was trimmed in a lighter shade of blue. It was nothing fancy — no lace or frills — but it had been a new dress made of a fabric which would be warmer than cotton during the upcoming winter. The second package had contained a new pair of shoes . . . black with small brass buckles. After having opened both packages, she had looked thoughtfully at the two men, but had been unable to speak immediately.

'Well,' the old man had asked defensively, 'a girl can't very well go looking fer a job wearing buckskins and a ole pair of mule-ear boots nor moccasins, now can she?'

'I don't know how I can ever thank the both of you for all you've done for me,' she had told them, while choking back the tears. 'You've been so kind to me. I'll never forget you, Antelope Horn, Ezekiel Zimmerman.'

Supper had been prepared and they had sat next to the fire and eaten. 'OK, missy, I'm gonna say this just one more time.' Then he had hesitated long enough to take another sip from his cup. 'Like I've done told ya before, me and ole Horn wanta give ya the money to get ya where ya wanta go and enough to tide ya over fer a while. We've got more than plenty to do us and we wish you'd take what little bit we're offering.' Then he had softly added with a wink, 'You'd be making two old men mighty happy.'

She had appreciated their sincere generosity and had known that she was probably being foolish to deny their offer, but she was proud and headstrong and once again refused to take it.

The old man had lowered his head, but had continued to smile at the girl's grit. He had known many women in his lifetime. There had been those whom he had known while growing up in Tennessee — tough women, used to the hard life of carving out a living in those rugged mountains. And there had been those he had known while in Lynch-burg and in the military . . . soft, city women, who loved to dance, sip tea and flirt with the young, handsome officers. But he had never in all of his years met a woman with the grit and determina-tion that this girl possessed. Had she been his own daughter, he could not have been more proud of her.

He had shaken his head upon her refusal. 'All right then, girlie. I reckon the only thing I can do fer ya is to help ya find yourself a job. So, while I's buying your new duds, I told the lady that made your dress — Mrs Oberman her name is — about our offer of giving ya the money; and I told her you's pigheaded and that you'd probably not take it. So, she told me, that if you's any good at sewing, she'd like fer ya to come by her place tomorrow and talk to her about working in her shop . . . maybe live there with her, too. Said she'd enjoy the company and that she had an extra room where you could sleep. Said that she needed the help, too, so y'all might be able to help each other.'

Emotions had run high that evening in the small camp along the North Platte. The old man and Antelope Horn had been happy that they had been able to assist the girl in evading her pursuers and had then helped her find a job. The girl had been happy for all of the same reasons.

The next morning, Maggie had donned her new blue dress and shoes, brushed her hair with a curry comb and had then placed the buckskins in a leather bag, which Antelope Horn had given her. As she had carefully placed the folded leather garments inside the bag, the thought had come to her that she would cherish those buckskins for the rest of her life, and she would wear them from time to time, just to remember.

When she was ready, the old man had walked with her to the dressmaker's house and had introduced the two women. Laura Oberman, a widow with no children, was a very pleasant lady. The three of them had sipped tea, while she and the girl had become acquainted. Talking and laughing together, the two women had become instant friends. Once certain that the girl would be happy there, the old man had walked back along the dry, dusty street and had rejoined the Sioux, who was already breaking their camp.

The old man had insisted that Maggie not sell her horse, just in case she might have need of it, and she had agreed to keep the animal until she was ready to move on. He had boarded the girl's horse at the livery; six months' board had been paid in advance and he had made arrangements with the hostler to pay for any extra expense that might be incurred upon their return to Casper in the spring. Finally, the two old men had crossed the North Platte via the bridge and had ridden north-by-northwest, toward the Big Horns and home.

That night in their camp, made in an outcropping of rocks on the open prairie, the two men had quietly sat by the fire after eating. Antelope Horn had smoked his long pipe, occasionally waving the smoke over his face and hair. The old man had dipped his snuff, drank his coffee and searched the clear night sky for the constellations. The night had been cold and they had sat near the fire, each deep in his own thoughts. The old man had been concerned that winter would soon be upon them. His old hip wound had been aching for the past few days; it had, for the past several years, become the signal that winter was near. As he had squirmed to reposition himself and rubbed his throbbing hip, it had brought back to mind the period of time during which he had been wounded.

He had grown up in the Appalachian Mountains, a day's ride west of the settlement known as Johnson's Depot, which had eventually been renamed Johnson City, Tennessee. His parents had met in Lynchburg, Virginia, where his mother's family had owned a number of businesses, including two large tobacco warehouses; they had been quite wealthy. Although as a youngster he had preferred to roam the mountains, hunting and fishing with his friends, and generally do nothing that his parents had regarded as constructive, his mother had insisted that he learn to read, write and become proficient in mathematics. He had been most defiant, but after considerable debate, they had eventually reached a compromise; as long as he had maintained good marks in his studies, he had been allowed to roam the hills during the day and had studied at night. Reading and writing had come easily to him, for he dearly loved reading of peoples and places of distant lands and times long past. But more than once his mother had been forced to threaten him with confinement to the house until he had shown improvement in his mathematics. When he had finally realized that he had no choice but to abide by his agreement to learn the math, he had concentrated more on his lessons and had shown himself to be an intelligent youngster and a quick learner. When he had finally completed the studies taught by his mother and was prepared for college, he had been sent to her family in Lynchburg, who had arranged his enrolment at the school of their choosing.

Having graduated in 1846 from the Virginia Military Institute in Lexington, Ezekiel Zimmerman had received a commission into the US military. By making the most of his charismatic personality and innate ability in matters involving military strategy, it took only a short time for him to gain the trust, respect and admiration of his superiors — and by using that same charisma and his boyish good looks, he had gained the admiration of their wives and daughters as well. He had been determined not to use his family's considerable influence to gain advancement. However, eventually his superior officers had become aware of the amount and extent of the attention given him by their ladies.

So, it had been no surprise when, a few months after the beginning of the first Schleswig-Holstein War, with the rank of captain, he had been dispatched, by military intelligence, on a top secret mission to Europe, attached as the aide to the unofficial United States military adviser and liaison to Denmark — who just happened to be a widower.

The Danes and Germans had been fighting over the region known as Schleswig-Holstein since the spring of 1848. A treaty had been signed in August of that year, but fighting had resumed the following January. The King of Denmark had immediately requested aid from the US Ambassador and the adviser had been dispatched straight away.

Ezekiel had arrived in Denmark at the end of February, 1849. Being young in years, only twenty-four years of age, relatively new to the military and anxious to make his name known in military circles, he had immediately suggested that he be sent to a forward position where he could observe the troops and assess the battles firsthand. The suggestion had been deemed astute. He had joined the forces of Danish General Christian Julius de Meza and had immediately requested to be attached to a front-line cavalry division. General de Meza had initially refused him, but the eager young captain's request had eventually been granted.

Through the month of April, he had commanded his company of cavalry. His unit had been in the first wave of riders in the battle of Adsbol, where he had viciously, yet meticulously, sliced and thrust with his saber as the thundering, screaming wall of mounted soldiers crashed through the Schleswig-Holstein line. At Dybbol where they had defeated the Saxons, he had been involved in the planning of the Danish battle strategy, but he had not been allowed to participate in the actual attack. By mid-May he had been awarded a field promotion to major, rewarding his brilliance in planning the Danish battle strategies, his ability to command his troops and his utter ferocity in their battles.

On 31 May, after assisting with the formation of their battle plan, he had led his cavalry unit in the fighting at Vejlby. The Danish forces were winning and the battle was nearly over when he had been struck in the side, just above his left hip, by a Prussian minie-ball. He had been immediately placed inside General de Meza's ambulance and carried to the field hospital where he had received care for his wound.

The lead ball had fractured his pelvis and had become lodged, requiring surgery to achieve its removal. During the days that had followed, the wound had become infected; on more than one occasion, the doctors had believed that he would not live. After five days of suffering from high fever and delirium, he had been transported by ambulance to the hospital in Copenhagen, where he had been treated and looked after by the king's personal physicians.

Finally, after four months and with constant intensive care, his wound was healing satisfactorily and eventually he had begun to regain his strength. He had just begun to walk without assistance, when, in mid-October, he had been summoned by his US commanding officer and ordered to return home. After having lodged considerable protest, he had sorrowfully boarded a ship bound for America.

Immediately upon his return to Washington, he had been examined by army doctors and hospitalized once more. Another four months of hospitalization passed before he had been told that his fighting days in the military were over, he would be assigned a position in Washington as an aide to some general, or as the commander of some out-of-the-way post, or he could resign his commission. But he was a warrior who loved and craved the challenge, excitement and heat of battle. So, after having given the matter but little thought, he had resigned his commission and, in the spring of 1850, immediately departed for the western frontier. That had been over twenty-five years earlier.

The old man, his eyes still glued to the stars, had still been reminiscing when Antelope Horn's voice had suddenly brought him back to the present. 'I will miss that girl.'

The old man had lowered his gaze once more to his companion and chuckled. 'Yep. She's a keeper, all right. I reckon we'll come back down early in the spring and check on her. Whatcha think, Horn?' The old Sioux had simply grunted his agreement.

7

Alvin Harding had, of course, not found the girl in Sheridan. He had, however, spent nearly a week there and had obtained information regarding an old man and Indian who lived somewhere in the Big Horn Mountains. The man with whom he had spoken had no idea where they could be found, only that they were there — somewhere.

The informant had said that they were considered to be 'like ghosts who moved on the mountains'; the stories that were told were something like tales he had heard as a child. More than once men had gone looking for them, hoping to find the source of the two old men's money, but none of those men had ever returned, or been heard from again . . . not one man. Whether they had met their doom, or had simply given up and moved on, the teller of the story had no idea, but the two old men were there; he had seen them twice, over the years, when they had ventured into town to trade . . . and they had money.

They kept to themselves most of the time, only being seen from time to time once or twice a year. So far as he knew, they never went to the same town twice in a row. Instead, they would be seen in one settlement or another, Sheridan then Buffalo, or Casper, then the trading post at the place known to the Indians as Ten Sleeps. They might appear anywhere, sell their furs and purchase a few provisions, then slip away unnoticed without saying a word to anyone.

The old Indian, a Sioux, he knew absolutely nothing about, but considered him a savage. The old man, known around Sheridan only as the Dutchman, was said to have been a soldier at one time. The stories were that he had fought somewhere in Europe back in the '40s and was considered to be a very dangerous man with both rifle and blade. The man telling the story had no firsthand knowledge, of course, but suggested that since those who had gone looking for the two mountain men had never returned, he would consider the stories of the old men to be more fact than fable.

Harding had been angered, thinking he had lost the girl to an old man and a savage Indian. He believed himself to be intelligent, fast with a gun and simply better than any old man — and especially some red savage. But he had finally departed from Sheridan and had ridden south to Buffalo, where he had rejoined the rest of his party.

It had galled Harding that he must depend on someone's skills other than his own to find Maggie Buckner. He had grown up helping his father in his mercantile store and had hated every minute that he had spent there. While the other boys were playing, fishing and hunting, he had been forced by his father to work in the store. Whenever he had suggested that he would rather be out of doors with his friends, his father had rebuked him, insisting that he put frivolous activities out of his mind. After all, Alvin was a city boy and would not be making his living by fishing or hunting.

'Alvin,' his father would scold, 'concentrate on your education, first. Learn to read well and to write properly, how to figure numbers and all else that you can. Then, keep your mind on your trade and learn this business. This store makes a very good living for us. Some day it will be yours to own and operate, so make it grow and you will prosper.' Young Alvin had grown to hate the store and he had learned to hate his father as well.

Then his father had died suddenly at the age of thirty-nine. There had been no prolonged illness. In fact, other than an occasional sniffle, the man had never been ill in his life and was considered to have been as healthy as an ox; his doctor had been quite surprised, even puzzled, at the man's death.

His father's will had provided that ownership of the store be transferred to Alvin, who was by then nineteen years of age. The family home and the remainder of his estate were left to Alvin's mother and siblings. Except for what the store might earn, Alvin had considered himself left virtually penniless.

His mother had remarried six months after his father's death. Until she had remarried, Alvin had felt at least some responsibility for her; once she had a new husband, he had felt responsible no longer.

He had abruptly sold the mercantile, settling for much less than its actual value, and had set out for the West. With his younger brother, cousin and two friends riding with him, twenty-year-old Alvin Harding had been a threat to anyone who might have stepped into his path.

In Madison, Indiana, they had been joined by three friends of Ben Anderson's, Kevin Love and his cousins

James and Charles Emerson, whose fathers had been an engineer and a brakeman on the Indianapolis & Madison Railroad. Love and the Emerson bothers had been running on the wrong side of the law since in their early teens and had been arrested in nearly every town along the Ohio River from Cincinnati to Evansville. With no plans other than traveling to California, the group of eight young men had ridden west; what they would do once there, they had not considered.

Alvin had begun the journey with his pockets full of money, so the group had lived foot-loose and fancy-free, for a while anyway. Whether in a roadside tavern or trading post in the smallest of settlements in Arkansas, or in the most elaborate hotel or saloon in Fort Worth, the money had flowed like water. He had paid for their meals, bought the drinks and paid for the women.

But soon the money had run low and they had begun to look for cattle or horses to steal and for isolated trading posts or stores to rob. Within only a few months of leaving Cincinnati, the group had been riding the outlaw trail. They had become wanted by the law in four states; in two of those states, they had committed hanging offenses. Those offenses included Love's being wanted for murdering a barmaid, when she had refused to retire to his room with him, and Alvin Harding for killing an unarmed gambler whom he had accused of cheating at cards.

Eventually, they had made their way to Las Cruses, New Mexico where Harding had overheard some men in a saloon talking about gold in the Black Hills of South Dakota and they had immediately set out for Deadwood. Alvin had told the other members of his group that he could see them all becoming rich, but whether their fortunes would come from their finding gold or by their stealing it, he had not said.

Three times, in the timber-covered hills south of Deadwood, they had come upon gold seekers working their claims. They had murdered all of those prospectors, numbering six men in total, and had taken what gold each had which amounted to a tidy sum. Eventually they had reached Lead, where he had made the deal with Buckner for his daughter.

But, after having lost the girl, Alvin had demanded they search for her; his ego would not allow him to be denied that which belonged to him. On the ride from Sheridan to Buffalo, he had not stopped looking; he had only suspended the search for the winter. He decided to return to Wyoming in the spring and eventually track down Maggie Buckner if it were the last thing he ever did.

After he had rejoined his men in Buffalo, the group had ridden south. For the next few weeks Harding had sought any information available about the old man and Indian who lived somewhere in the Big Horns. After stopping for several days at Fort

Laramie, and then spending two weeks in Cheyenne, they had eventually reached Denver in early November. Although several times during their stay one or more of the group had been a regular guest of Denver's town marshal, they had spent the winter by drinking, playing cards and patronizing the sporting houses.

During those five months, the thought of losing the girl had simmered in Alvin's mind. Liquor had only fueled the flames of his anger, and the sporting girls only served to somehow remind him of Maggie. Night after night he had sat and brooded. His moodiness had finally caused his cousin Ben to become concerned about his sanity. When they had once again ridden north from Denver in mid-April, their money was nearly gone and Alvin Harding was even more obsessed by the thought that he had lost the girl to an old man and a savage redskin. On several occasions, especially when drinking, he had ranted and raved about the girl, his face twisted with anger and hatred.

On more than one occasion Ben had considered leaving the group; he had thought of simply slipping away during one of their drunken bouts. He was convinced that Alvin was hopelessly insane and would sooner or later be the death of them all.

8

Only a few nights after the old man and Indian had returned to their cabin, snow had once again fallen upon the Big Horns. They had gathered their straying livestock and prepared their traps for their winter's work.

Every evening as they had checked and repaired the traps and discussed their trap lines, the subject of the girl had always arisen. Both men had grown to like her very much and wished for her a better life than she had lived with her father. By the time they had begun to lay their traps, the subject of the girl only rose once or twice a week, but she was always in their thoughts.

By late November their traps had been laid. They had covered the area around the cabin for nearly five miles, placing traps in beaver ponds, along streams and near burrows where they had seen signs of beaver, mink and other fur-bearing animals.

By the end of February, they had collected a sizeable number of pelts, and they had pulled their traps by the middle of March. Although it meant going to the same settlement twice in a row, they would take some of their plunder to Casper and trade for the provisions they needed. Both men had been anxious to see the girl again.

Although April was much earlier than they had ever left their cabin to sell their furs and would mean having to tramp through snow that might still be quite deep in places, the old man and Antelope Horn had ridden south through the Big Horns toward the small town along the North Platte. Travel was indeed difficult and slow while still in the mountains, so it had taken them an extra two days to make the trip. Five days after leaving the cabin they had crossed Louis Guinard's bridge and had made their camp under the same lone pine where they had camped the previous fall. Both men had wanted to know how the girl had fared through the winter and both had hoped that she had not already left for Oregon.

Once the animals had been seen to and a fire had been laid, the two old men had walked down the street to the dressmaker's. When they had entered Laura Oberman's shop, the girl had at once greeted both men with a heartfelt, animated hug. Before leaving her to return to their camp, she had insisted they return for supper and they had graciously accepted her invitation.

On the second morning after their arrival, they had gone about their business of selling and trading their furs. Then they met the girl at noon to have lunch at a small restaurant/saloon a few doors up the street from the dressmaker's shop.

'So, how did you two do this winter? Did you collect plenty of hides and furs?'

The old man had smiled in delight that the girl was so thoughtful as to ask about their business. Many times it had been in his thoughts that he would be proud had she been his daughter. He had suddenly found himself wishing that he were thirty years younger but had then thought himself an old fool, and he had chuckled. 'We did just fine, missy. We brought a few down to trade with, but we'll bale the rest of them furs up in a few weeks. I reckon they'll bring a tidy sum; probably enough to provide us with provisions fer a couple of years or so. How'd your winter go? Do ya have enough money fer your trip?'

She had answered his question between spoonfuls of buffalo stew. 'I already have enough money for my trip and then some. Mrs Oberman has paid me a very good wage . . . more than I really deserve, I think. Since she didn't charge me for the room and we shared our food expenses, I've been able to save nearly two hundred and seventy dollars. I've already priced a ticket to Eugene, but I'll have to purchase a ticket from there down to Ashland; it's on the route from Portland to Sacramento.

'But, well, I really like it here in Casper, I've made several friends — Mrs Oberman, Mr and Mrs Combs — he's the man who runs the stage station and his wife — and their son, Tim. There's others who have been quite friendly, but I've gotten to be very good friends with those folks I just mentioned.'

The old man had smiled that wry smile once more; he had already detected the reluctance to leave in the girl's voice. 'The Combs, huh? I know Dub, Mr Combs, and his missus. They're good folks. I reckon young Tim's a pretty good feller, too, although he's just a youngster.'

'He's not so young,' the girl had retorted. 'He's nineteen, and he makes a good living working for the stage line.'

The old man knew the Combs family very well. He and Dub Combs had become friends many years before, after Combs had opened the stage station near the old fort. Over the years, when in Casper, the old man and Antelope Horn had eaten many meals at the Combs' table. As far as young Tim was concerned, the old man considered him a fine young man. As a youngster, he had talked with Ezekiel at length about the life of a mountain man and the collecting of furs and hides. Tim had visited their cabin many times when he and his father had come to hunt with the old man and the Indian. He remembered seeing the longing and excitement in the boy's eyes as they had stalked their prey. Tim had silently moved through the timber with stealth and knowing. On more than one occasion, the old man had remarked to the boy's father, while they had watched him make his stalk, that the youngster 'takes to the mountains like a lone curly wolf.' His dad had replied that, if his son had not felt obligated to help operate the station, he believed he would leave home and seek his own way in just such a location.

While they had eaten, the girl had continued talking about her activities, the people whom she had met and the few clothes which she had obtained during her stay in Casper.

The old man had been certain that she was prepared to make her journey to Oregon, if she chose to go. But he never told her that, when the three had arrived in Casper the previous autumn, he had asked the dressmaker if she had need of an extra pair of hands at her shop. He never mentioned that she had told him, in fact, that she had less than enough business to keep her own hands busy. He neither told the girl that he had asked the favor of his friend Laura Oberman to allow the girl to stay with her and help her in the dress shop, nor that he had given the woman $300 with which to pay the girl's wages and board.

When they had finished their meal, the three had left the restaurant. Since saloons were known in the West as clearing houses of information the old man had decided to visit a nearby establishment, to see if he might gather any information about the passing and/or whereabouts of Harding's group. Since Antelope Horn was not permitted inside a saloon, he had accompanied the girl as she had done a bit of shopping.

At the Fremont Saloon he had talked with his old friend, an Irishman named Adam O'Rourke, the proprietor and bartender. O'Rourke had been at Fort Laramie during the previous autumn and remembered Harding and his group's passing through there on their way to Cheyenne. They had stayed in the town for only a few days, asking questions, first about the girl, then about an old man and an Indian who lived in the Big Horns.

When he had heard the mention of his old friends, O'Rourke had paid close attention to Harding. He had assured the old man that he had gotten no information from anyone who had been in that saloon, but he didn't know what they might have found out from someone else in town. 'When they pulled out I watched them to see which way they were headed. As soon as I got back to Casper, I made sure the girl was still safe with Mrs. Oberman.' The only thing that he had been able to add was that he had heard Harding tell one of the members of his group, that they would return north in the spring and attempt to locate the old man and Indian and to pick up the girl's trail.

Suddenly there had been a wary expression on the Irishman's face and his voice had taken on a much more serious tone. 'I'd watch out for that bunch, Zeke. None of them boys looked all that traveled, but they're a bloody bad bunch and that one they called Alvin had strange eyes. It was like he wasn't all there, even touched maybe . . . if you know what I mean. I've seen that girl around town this winter. Heard she came here from the diggings someplace in the Black Hills. I suppose there's a long story behind it — why those gents are looking for her and all — but she's a nice girl, according to them around town that knows her. I don't guess anybody here in Casper would want to see anything bad happen to her.' He spoke in an even lower tone as he leaned closer to the old man and added, 'But believe this, Zeke, he's as mean as a copperhead and he figures to have that girl, come hell or high water and that pack of bloodthirsty pups riding with him are as faithful as an old sooner dog.'

The old man had suddenly been uneasy. Had they returned to hunt for her before the girl left for Oregon, or before their return to Casper, she would have been abducted and forced to leave with them. He had immediately paid for his coffee and had been thanking O'Rourke for the information when he heard the shots.

Eight . . . nine shots, or more, had echoed down the street. As he had rushed through the door and into the street, he had heard the pounding of hoofs on the wooden bridge. He had quickly glanced in that direction, only to see Harding and his group turn west at the north end of the bridge and gallop away upstream along the North Platte — and Maggie was with them. John Talbot, the town's deputy, had been firing his revolver at the group, when the old man had insisted that he cease firing, for fear of Maggie being injured.

A crowd had already gathered outside the mercantile, when he had quickly walked up and parted the mass of humanity. There, on the ground only a few feet from the door of the store, as the earth around him was turning red with his blood, lay Antelope Horn; Dub Combs had knelt over him.

'Dub?'

Combs had raised his head and looked straight into his dark, fiery eyes. He shook his head. 'He's gone, Zeke.'

Raw fury had at once risen in the old man's chest. 'Look after him, will ya, Dub,' to which Combs nodded. Then,

119

as he had turned to go, he had added, 'And see after our animals for a few days, 'til I get back.'

Then, without waiting for a reply, with clenched teeth and a burning fire in his belly, the old man had turned and walked toward their camp, pushing his way through the growing crowd as he had passed.

He had saddled the grulla and put two weeks' supplies, along with a small skillet and coffee pot, into his saddlebags. Once his provisions were packed, he had retrieved his Remington Rolling Block Rifle and bandoleer from the pack-saddle, on which they had been tied, and stepped into leather. Without another word to Combs or to any of the others, the old man had walked the gelding across the bridge, turned west along the river and had spurred his mount to a lope.

Methodically he had followed their trail all that day, noting that whoever was leading the group was not totally certain as to the path they should take.

They had traveled nearly a mile north of the Oregon Trail, but their trail had wandered from time to time, causing the old man to change his plan of attack more than once.

Finally, after the group had made an early camp on the banks of Horse Creek east of Sentinel Rocks, as he had done so many years before in Denmark, the old man had formulated his battle plan. He had dared not rush their camp for he was severely outnumbered and he had feared the girl would be injured by stray gunfire; instead, he had decided that an ambush was his only recourse.

They had changed their direction an hour before they had stopped, causing him to believe that they would avoid the wagon trail completely whenever possible. He had decided that, in an effort to hide their trail from anyone who might be following, they planned to cross the Granites in the rough and rocky terrain of the mountain pass just north of Devil's Gate.

There had remained only a few minutes of daylight, when he saw the faint trail of smoke rising from among the cottonwoods near the mouth of Horse Creek. After locating their camp, he had left the grulla in a draw, nearly 400 yards east of the group's camp, and had walked to the top of the low ridge. Seated behind a clump of the abundant sagebrush as the dim light of dusk had faded, through his long glass the old man had watched the group mill around the camp. Maggie had remained tied while two of the men had prepared their meal and the other six men had sat around the fire drinking. Once it had become full dark, their fire was the only light that could be seen anywhere. When the light from that fire had become sufficient to light the camp, the old man had placed the long rifle across shooting sticks and had taken aim. Using the light from their fire to silhouette his sights, he gently squeezed the trigger. Fire belched from the rifle's muzzle as it delivered its deadly offering.

Turmoil had erupted instantly within the camp on the east bank of Horse Creek, north of the Sweetwater River. With one man down, men had scrambled for cover and the fire had been doused with water, total darkness had once again fallen upon the prairie. When he had returned and was mounted once more, the old man had remembered the sight of the men diving for cover and he had sounded a sinister chuckle.

The night air had been quite cool when he had ridden in an arc north of the place where the group had stopped; with no fire it would be a cold night in that camp. He had crossed Horse Creek nearly two miles upstream of their campsite and had ridden on through the night. In the cold darkness, while dragging a small clump of brush to eradicate any tracks he might leave, he had wound his way through the mountains, using the same pass that they would eventually be forced to use.

When daylight had again lighted the

broad rolling valley between the Wind River Range and the Antelope Hills known as South Pass, the old man had sat atop the pale-blue grulla on the narrow bench west of Savage Peaks, waiting. When the diminished group had ridden into range, he had again delivered his message of death, allowing the long barreled rifle to do his talking.

9

Now the old man sat quietly near his fire along Sheep Creek. Maggie Buckner and her four remaining captors were, he believed, only a few miles south of where he now camped. Would they chance building a fire? Since they had suffered the loss of a man the night before, he doubted it, but if not it would certainly be another cold night for them. This day had not been warm, but now the night air had grown much colder. He was disturbed by the thought of the girl having to spend the night without a coat to ward off the cold; it had been midday and warm when she had been abducted, so she had not been wearing one.

Would Alvin Harding harm the girl in any way? He hoped not but, according to O' Rourke, the man had been very angry after having been unable to find her. Should he change his plan and attack now, even though it would mean putting the girl at risk of being wounded in a gun battle? Finally, he decided that Harding would be so pleased that he once again had her in his possession, that he would not punish her in any way. But he might decide to molest her, and that the old man feared more than a beating. There were three other men with him, but would that matter to him? The old man quickly weighed the risk of waiting versus wading headlong into their camp and finally decided that she would be safe enough for the present — *at least that's what he forced himself to believe.*

The hour grew late and since the coffee pot was empty, the old man spat out his snuff, rolled up in his blankets and slept. But his dreams were not the pleasant dreams of laughing with the girl as those he had dreamed only a few nights before. Now he dreamed of gunshots, the beating of horses' hoofs and the lifeless body of his old friend and the blood-soaked ground beneath him.

★   ★   ★

Knowing that the old man must be camped only a short distance away, panic filled Alvin Harding as he stared into the fire of the quiet camp at the base of Sheep Mountain. For several months Ben Anderson had considered the possibility that his cousin was insane, but had he been there beside the fire watching him on this night, he would have been certain of it. The others lay near the fire curled in their blankets, but he sat on a log simply staring into the flickering embers. What would he do now? He must have a plan to procure more supplies and then to rid himself of the old man who followed them. Oh, he was certain that it was the old man; having heard what he had in Sheridan and the other towns, it had to be him.

In Sheridan they had told him that

the old man had in years past been a soldier in some war in Europe and was considered to be dangerous. At Fort Laramie, he had spoken with two men who claimed to know of the old man and his Sioux friend. They had said that it had been told around that both of the old men were capable of tracking a trout in a stream and, although the informants had no firsthand knowledge of his ever being in any sort of shooting fracas, it was said that the Dutchman was a very dangerous man, able to kill from long range; a fact which Harding had now observed first hand. He was also told that the old man never forgot a wrong that was done him and that the severity of his reprisal would be equal to the wrong ... and his group had killed the Indian, the old man's long-time friend and companion.

Then in Cheyenne, Harding had met someone who had actually met the old man. A former trapper turned buffalo hunter had spent the night with the two old men in the Big Horns and had told

Alvin the location of the cabin. But it had been late in the season and the weather conditions were capable of turning perilous at any time. With the possibility of a sudden snowfall trapping them in the mountains without food and shelter, Ben had refused to guide him in an attempt to search for the place. After considerable debate, Ben had finally convinced Alvin to forego further searching and continue on to Denver, then return to the Big Horns, if he must, in the spring.

They had now returned to Wyoming and recaptured the girl, but they were at present out of food and would have to obtain more before continuing the journey to Fort Bridger, of that he had no doubt. There was also no doubt in his mind that as long as the old man lived he would continue to hound them, for Alvin had already witnessed the extent of his reprisal.

He felt the panic welling up inside himself. His mind raced with ideas as perspiration formed on his brow. He gave thought of immediately hunting down his pursuer and killing him, but Alvin quickly put it from his mind. Where would he look for him? The old man knew this country well and he knew nothing of it. Then, suddenly, Alvin gave thought to releasing the girl. If he turned her loose the old man would forget about him and his depleted group and see her back to Casper — or would he? What was it the men in Fort Laramie had told him? 'The old man never forgets a wrong that's done him', was what they had said. They had taken Maggie Buckner from under his nose and killed his friend. If what the men at the fort had told him about the old man living by the feud was true, he would never stop hunting them, not until the four remaining men of the group were dead.

Alvin was frightened. Beads of sweat streamed over his temples and tears were suddenly in his eyes. How would they find their way? Ben had been their guide and, although he had been over the trail from Salt Lake to the Pacific Ocean only once, he had known some of the trails and had been given directions and seen the maps. How would they now get to California? How would they get through these mountains? How would they escape from that malicious old man?

Suddenly, as quickly as Alvin had lost his composure he regained it. He could do it; he could get them through. He would first ride south and find Green River, of which he had been told, instead of South Pass City, hoping to throw the old man off their trail. There he would get explicit directions to Fort Bridger, or perhaps some town to the south in Utah; there were several directions he could travel from Green River by which he could lose that old man. Once he made it to the next town, he would get more directions and have someone draw him a map that showed the way for as far as they knew it. He would repeat that same process until they reached their destination. He could do it; he *would* do it. He continued to stare into the fire and his mind continued to race as he turned his current situation over and over in his head.

He was tired, but sleep would not come for him. Twice he lay in his blankets hopelessly attempting to fall asleep, but both times he abandoned the attempt, sat up and smoked. It was cold and getting colder. Although it might mean revealing their location and being shot at again, he piled wood on the fire hoping to rid himself of the chill deep within him; it never left him, but he was wet with sweat. Was it the cold of the night, or the cold chill of fear that made his body shiver? Finally, the sky turned gray as daylight approached and he filled the small pot with water and poured into it the last handful of coffee from the sack that he kept in his saddle-bag.

As the water boiled he roused the four sleeping bodies which lay around the fire into sitting upright. They each rubbed their eyes, forcing themselves to prepare for another grueling day of riding. When they had finished their breakfast of coffee and jerky, they rode away from the small camp on Sheep Creek. Displaying a veneer of confidence, Alvin led them around the western end of Sheep Mountain then turned south, all the while hoping he would be able to find Green River and more supplies.

* * *

Harding was still seated near his fire and pondering his situation, when the old man woke well before dawn. He saw to the animals, then prepared and ate his breakfast. As he finished the last drops of the coffee, the sun was pushing the dark veil of night westward with the gray line of dawn. When his fire had been extinguished he mounted and rode south along Sheep Creek toward the place where he expected Harding's group to have camped; in the swirling cold wind, he smelled it long before he found it. Cautiously, he quietly approached the camp, his Henry held ready in his right hand, finally stopping beside a thick cottonwood. A thin finger of smoke rose from the dying coals as he sat among the trees some forty yards downstream from the campsite.

He sat atop the grulla searching the camp and the surrounding timber. The camp was empty, but he had expected that. After a few minutes he walked the tall grulla to the edge of the dead camp and drew up once more. The horse was alert, his dark head up and his ears pricked forward; he tossed his head and blew as they approached the smoldering coals.

'Easy, Buster, they've already lit out. I just wanta have me a look around.'

The old man slid the rifle back into the scabbard and stepped down from the saddle to survey the camp. There was nothing to be found that would help him trail his quarry, but he found what he was looking for. He searched for any blood on the ground, but found none. The ground was undisturbed, except for the grass that had been mashed down by the normal movement around the camp. He was certain that the girl would fight any assailant if she were attacked, but there was nothing to suggest a struggle had taken place. He saw where she had slept, close to the fire near three others, but there was no evidence to suggest that she had been harmed.

He also found where the man had sat on the log near the fire. Judging by the signs left by that man, he had spent a sleepless night. The grass had been trampled and mashed with much of it being broken off or pulled out by its roots, leaving the old man to surmise that this man was troubled and restless. He knew somehow that this man was Alvin Harding. 'He's already losing sleep,' he thought aloud.

The old man was still squatting, studying the areas around the fire, when he heard the faint and distant sound of a horse slowly approaching through the timber from the direction of his camp of the night before.

Quickly he rose and retrieved his Henry from its scabbard. Then he quietly crossed the creek and cautiously made his way downstream toward the soft hoofbeats. He squatted behind a small willow tree and allowed the horse and rider to pass by. With the stealth of a mountain cat the old man slipped from behind the willow, crossed the creek again and silently followed the horse and rider until they neared the camp and stopped beside the grulla.

'Mr Zimmerman?' the rider called softly.

'You need to be more careful, Tim boy. If I'd been one of that bunch, right about now you'd be bleeding all over that fine saddle.'

Tim Combs was so startled when he heard the voice that he nearly fell off of his horse. 'Lord Almighty, Mr Zimmerman, you scared me outta ten years' growth.'

Normally the old man would have found humor in the boy's statement, but right then he was more irritated than amused. 'Whatcha doing here, Tim?' he asked gruffly.

Without hesitation Tim answered, 'I've come to help you get Maggie — er Miss Buckner — back from those men. I started to join you right away, but, well, it took some talking to convince Mom and Dad that you'd need help. Dad still didn't think so, but he finally conceded and gave me the okay to follow you. I started out tracking that bunch that took her and came across a fresh grave over on Horse Creek yesterday morning; then I found three of them, yesterday evening, lying dead out there this side of Devil's Gate. I knew that had to be your work, so I picked up your trail and followed it from there. I spent the night a few miles north of here, got up early and found where you spent last night, then just followed your tracks up this creek.' Then Tim straightened himself and sat up proudly. 'I'm here to help you, Mr Zimmerman. What do we do next?' The old man started to protest, but Tim interrupted, 'No need to tell me to go home, sir. I told my folks I's gonna help you find her and get her back and that's what I intend to do.'

The old man smiled involuntarily at the young man's tenacity. 'Okay, Tim boy, we'll go together. Fer now, you circle around yonder and see if ya can pick up their trail. I just wantta give this camp one more look-see.'

Tim reined his paint to his right, crossed the creek and circled the camp looking for the tracks of the four riders who had spent the night there. The old man returned to his spot just outside the circle of trampled grass and spent a few more minutes studying the signs. Finally, having gathered all of the information that could be had from the camp, the old man remounted and followed after his young friend.

10

The sky was dark with heavy clouds and the wind blew increasingly stronger as Alvin Harding led the group away from the Green Mountains. He rode south over the rolling, broken prairie toward the Antelope Hills and the small town of Green River. The dark, ominous clouds steadily rolled over the snowcapped peaks of the distant mountains on his right; a storm was inevitable. It had been cold all through the night, but now the temperature was steadily dropping even lower. Even though it was the end of April, he feared they were about to suffer the life-threatening effects of a Wyoming snowstorm, of which he had been told several frightening stories.

He had only a remote idea of how far Green River was from where they now were, but he knew that they could not stop out on the open ground over which they now rode. They must find shelter and the small town, which had been built on the banks of the river for which it had been named, was the only shelter that he could settle for. Sweetwater Station was somewhere behind them to the north, but to ride there was to ride back toward the old man and certain danger. Their survival would depend on his finding Green River.

Along they rode, five riders hunch-backed over their saddle horns against the biting wind, which touched them like icy fingers. The four men wore heavy coats, but the girl had only a wool blanket wrapped around her shoulders to stave off the bitter cold. They had been riding for just over an hour when the first snowflakes fell. Large, wet crystals of ice stuck to their coats, hats and her blanket. Within minutes of those first flakes the snow blew over them in heavy, blinding gales, blotting out the landscape and allowing them to see for only a few yards. Sam

Ferguson handed his slicker over to Maggie and she pulled it on over her head, wearing it outside the heavy blanket to keep it dry.

Almost immediately the now frozen ground turned white and the limbs and leaves of the sagebrush, junipers and piñons became covered with the heavy, white crystals. On they plodded as the snow grew deeper, heads bowed and hats pulled low over their watering eyes in defense against the brutal wind.

Suddenly an idea struck Alvin like a clapper ringing a bell. The snow would certainly cover their tracks, he thought, and the tracks which they had left since leaving their camp on Sheep Creek would lead the old man south, convincing him that they were bound for Green River. Immediately he decided to turn west for South Pass City and that's just what he did.

As Alvin turned the small column west and informed the others of his decision, Maggie felt more desperate than ever. She was certain that the old man was behind them, somewhere, but she was certain that he would lose their trail in the deepening snow and would not know of Harding's change in direction. She suddenly realized that she must do something to help him find her. But what?

The group rode for hours and the snow grew deeper as they rode, causing their horses to struggle at times. Having spent but little time in the region, no one in the group, including Maggie Buckner, had ever seen a blizzard such as this one. They had been riding across the wind as they had ridden south, but now they rode directly into it and it snipped at their faces like an icy chisel. 'Dang it, Alvin!' protested his brother Arnold. 'We've got to get inside outta this blasted weather.'

'The only place I know of around here is South Pass City. If you think you can come up with someplace closer, just lead the way. I'll be right behind you.'

Alvin's response had been harsh, so

after that no one spoke. They ripped pieces of cloth from the tails of their coats and her blanket wrapping their burning, frostbitten fingers and they each wiggled their toes, as they rode, to keep them from freezing. The snow landed on their faces and their cheeks and noses smarted and tingled with the onset of frostbite. Alvin thought of stopping to build a fire, but even if they could find wood in this place where only the sagebrush grew, it would not be dry enough to burn. He could only ride on and hope that he could locate South Pass City before they froze.

By midday they had ridden into the foothills of the Wind River Mountains. The snow was already nearly knee deep on the horses in most places and, due to drifting, belly deep in the some of the draws. The rocks and shale were covered by the white mass, making the steep banks of the gullies and washes slick, difficult to navigate and dangerous. Several times a horse went to its knees and then struggled, and even needed help, to stand again. Every step the horses took could lead to a fall, injury and even death for both horse and rider; every member of the party knew that if they lost their horses death would be imminent.

Finally, late in the afternoon with sundown only a short time away, they climbed out of a deep draw, rode up the side of a low hill and stopped on the crest of the ridge near the upper end of a valley so that Alvin could attempt to get his bearings. He searched frantically, but through the falling, blowing snow he could barely see that below them the narrow valley lay to the south and in its bottom he could occasionally make out a small creek. He knew that the tree-covered Wind River Mountains lay snow-covered and impassable to the north, but they were made invisible by the wall of frozen precipitation. He was certain, from all he had been told, that South Pass could not be far from where they sat. Alvin Harding squinted his watering eyes against the biting wind and searched for any sign of a trail.

Suddenly Sam Ferguson sat bolt upright, stood in his stirrups and excitedly pointed. As he peered out from under the frozen brim of his hat, through the falling snow, he saw the faint outline of a building. 'It's right down there, Alvin.'

'Where?'

Momentarily forgetting the icy blowing snow in his excited state, Sam still stood in his stirrups as he pointed. 'Down there! Down there!'

Gold had been discovered in a nearby creek sometime in 1842 and the settlement of South Pass City was built almost immediately. The early settlers had been forced to defend themselves against frequent attacks by the Cheyenne and Sioux, but the small town had grown steadily. By 1870, it had become a major mining town and the population had been estimated to be 4,000 residents. Although some of the people had moved on to find their fortunes elsewhere, as the five riders approached from the top of the ridge, it was still a sizeable town.

Alvin knew that he was taking an enormous chance on Maggie attempting to find help to escape him in such a place, but he saw no alternative and was forced to risk it. They angled their way down the hillside, carefully, slowly walking their horses. The town was only a quarter of a mile from where they had sat on the ridge, but because of the heavy blowing snow Harding had not been able to see the gray shadowy form of any of the buildings. To the five riders it seemed as if it took an eternity to descend the hillside, but in only a few minutes, they were in South Pass City and stepping down near the front doors of the Black Horse Livery. Arnold Harding opened the doors and they led their animals inside.

The hostler motioned toward some empty stalls along the north wall. 'Just put your horses in them stalls, boys. Grain's in the bin; I'll throw some hay down for them.' He climbed the ladder and from the loft he forked down copious portions of the dry alfalfa to each of their mounts. 'Mighty bad weather to be traveling in. Where you folks headed?'

Harding gave Maggie a hard look, again warning her with his eyes to say nothing that would cause trouble. 'California. We're new to this county. Can you recommend an easy route? My wife here has found the going through the mountains sort of rough.'

The hostler chuckled, but kept forking the hay. 'Well, I reckon the wagon road is the easiest way; them mountain trails will all be impassable, now. There's always the slight possibility of Indian troubles, but once ya get over past Salt Lake you oughta be all right.'

'Is there someplace here in town where we can put up for a couple of days?'

'Sure is. The Idaho House Hotel, up the street there, is as good as they come . . . good food, too. They got theirselves a German woman for a cook and she's a dandy, makes the best dang strudel you ever sunk your teeth into.'

Harding roughly grasped Maggie by the upper arm and led her from the livery with Arnold, Jim and Sam trailing them. 'You keep your mouth shut, Maggie. Otherwise, you're apt to get somebody killed.' Through the heavy snow they walked to the hotel where Alvin paid for their rooms, then led the group to the dining room.

Maggie feared that the old man could no longer help her because the snow had come so quickly and had piled itself to such a depth; he would certainly lose their trail in the storm. So, while they ordered their food, she searched the room for anyone from whom she might seek assistance to escape the clutches of Alvin Harding. But a hurried glance around the room told her that she would find no one there who could help her; there were only two middle-aged businessmen seated and having their meals and they appeared to be unarmed. She could only continue to bide her time.

After they had eaten a quiet supper, the five members of the party walked up the stairs to their rooms. Once inside, Alvin glared at Maggie with animal lust in his eyes and a sinister smile on his lips. But before he could say a word or move toward her she issued a warning of her own. 'If you try anything, Alvin, I'll scream my blasted head off. I'll raise such a ruckus that we'll have everybody in this hotel up here and they'll string you up to the nearest tree. You leave me alone and I'll not cause you any problems.'

For a few seconds he hesitated. At that moment, if he had to strike a deal with the Devil to keep her quiet, he would. 'Okay, Maggie, I'll bide my time. But sooner or later, I'll have you: that old man will never be able to keep that from happening.'

★ ★ ★

The temperature continued to drop as if pulled down by an anchor and the dark, ominous clouds rolled over the peaks of the Wind River Range. The snow came, just as the old man knew that it would. He followed their tracks until they disappeared beneath the deepening white blanket; those tracks had pointed the way toward Green River. As he and Tim continued to ride south he could see that the boy was having a hard time of it, but it was the boy who had noticed the strange horizontal line of snow and ice suspended between the two clumps of sagebrush.

'Mr Zimmerman! Look at that.'

The old man watched as Tim walked his horse the couple of yards west of their path, pulled the lariat off of the brush and shook it to remove the snow and ice.

'Which way was that rope lying, Tim?'

The boy hesitated for a few seconds, but then realized what the rope represented. 'East and west, sir.' He watched the old man through squinted eyes, in an attempt to read his mind. 'You thinking that Maggie left this for us?'

The old man was apprehensive and shook his head. 'I ain't fer sure, Tim. Maybe, but it could have been left to make us think they've changed their course again and throw us off.'

They continued to ride south through the storm, Tim wearing too light a coat and being more and more affected by the cold. With his young friend in mind, the old man searched his memory and soon recalled an overhang along the north face of the Beaver Rim, only a short distance from where they now rode. It was deep enough to provide shelter for them both, as well as for their animals and from there, if the weather co-operated, they could reach Green River late in the afternoon of the following day.

The overhang was difficult to find in the blowing snow, but after a bit of searching he finally located it. While

Tim stripped and rubbed down the horses with the saddle blankets, the old man built a larger than normal fire at one end, where there was protection from the wind by a natural rock formation. More than once passers-by, including the old man himself, had built their fires here and it appeared that most of those who had camped here had dragged deadfalls under the protective overhang for future use; having dry wood for their fire would not be a problem. Coffee was on and there was meat in the skillet before either man said a word.

'Mr Zimmerman, do you think she'll be all right in this weather?'

The old man hesitated before looking into the young man's eyes. 'I venture they've put up in someplace like this one here, somewheres down in the Divide Basin. It'll probably quit snowing before long and the temperature'll climb back up again. They'll probably head on down to Green River come morning, pick up what supplies they'll need and move on.' He hesitated again, then added, 'I'd say she's fine, Tim boy. She's a tough little gal. She'll do what she has to do to survive.'

The old man once more searched his memory, this time for a place where Harding's group could find refuge from the blizzard. He knew of a cave a quarter of the way up the eastern slope of Five Finger Butte and two other very good places south of the Red Desert, but he doubted that anyone of Harding's lot would have knowledge of any of them or any others for that matter. He was still contemplating their plight when he suddenly remembered the rope.

Maggie had shown herself to be savvy enough to have thought of leaving such a sign, but had she in fact left the rope there? Just how smart was Alvin Harding? How much knowledge of this country did he possess? He had not shown himself to be at all trail wise, but just how much did he know? Maybe enough, the old man thought, to attempt to lose his pursuer in the snowstorm. Green River would give Harding the opportunity to travel either west or south into Utah where the settlements were close enough to replenish his food stores without having to keep a large supply on hand. He could also travel east into Colorado and be able to reach Grand Junction in only a few days.

The old man was worried about Maggie. She didn't have a coat and the current weather conditions had taken their toll on a seasoned old man and boy who had been relatively prepared to endure a storm, but an unprepared girl — He forced himself to put the thought out of his mind temporarily as he stirred and added fuel to the fire. But something else kept pushing its way into the old man's head: his gut kept telling him that the rope had been intended to advise him of their having changed direction. Try as he might, he could not push the notion from his thoughts.

For as long as he had been able to follow them, the tracks had pointed south in a straight line and directly toward Green River, but then Tim had found that infernal lariat. Had Maggie indeed left the rope, or had Harding planted it there to throw him off of their trail? And there was also the possibility that it had been accidentally dropped from the saddle horn of some passing cowhand as he sloped his way across the Divide in search of strays, a job or simply riding the grub-line. Although it was a rare thing to happen, occasionally a 'puncher would simply lose his rope.

His gut, the girl's uncanny ability on the trail and the fortuitously discovered evidence kept telling him that Harding had turned west and headed for South Pass, once the snow had begun to cover his tracks. He continued to argue with himself that Green River gave the man a better chance to escape him, but they needed to find shelter and South Pass was at least half a day closer. But did

Harding know that?

If Harding thought that his pursuer was convinced that the group was bound for Green River and its multiple escape routes, would he not be confident that changing direction during the blizzard and riding to South Pass would be an even safer move? But in thinking that, might he not chance leaving the rope in hope that it would be discovered and convince his pursuer that he had changed direction, only to keep to his original trail?

But what had been the odds on him even seeing that rope? Unless he was only minutes behind Harding's group, the rope might be covered by the snow and invisible to any passer-by. And what if he rode farther away from their trail than he had? He would never have seen it. It had been an accident that they had in fact been so close to the trail as it was. Or were they even near the trail and that lone cowpuncher had simply dropped the dang thing. The old man's mind whirled with the same questions rolling over and over again in his mind. He had himself quite a dilemma.

He was still attempting to sort through the seemingly endless possibilities when they seated themselves near to the fire. As they ate they discussed what Harding might do next. The old man laid out his idea to Tim that Harding had turned west for South Pass; with any luck, they were already there and the girl was out of the storm. He also laid out the other possibilities for the young man to ponder.

But Tim firmly held to the thought that Maggie had been the one to leave the rope. Otherwise, why else would it have been uncoiled and placed, as it had been, atop the two widely spaced clumps of sagebrush? He believed that it had been left so intentionally, to get the old man's attention. The old man simply shook his head, but continued to discuss their options.

Now, if indeed they had reached the small town along the banks of Willow Creek, Harding would have the supplies that they would need to reach Fort Bridger. Without an experienced guide and considering the recent snowstorm the old man was certain that Harding would not chance crossing the mountains by way of Teton Pass, unless he was an even bigger fool than the old man suspected. The Mormon Trail would probably be his route and Fort Bridger would be his next destination. Eventually, they made their plans accordingly.

'I'm fairly confident that's where he's took them, Tim boy.'

'In for a penny, in for a pound. Maggie's smart, Mr Zimmerman. I think she would have thought to leave some sign and I believe she left that rope there for you to find. You make the call, Mr Zimmerman and I'll be with you all the way. From here we should be able to reach South Pass by noon tomorrow.'

'Yep, we could. But we ain't gonna foller them into town; we'll make our play out here in open country. Town's the last place I wanta catch up with that bunch. When I rain down what I've got planned fer Harding and them other three, I don't intend to have a bunch of witnesses standing 'round. Them town's folks would be hollering fer the law and a judge, jury and such . . . and other than their Maker, I intend to be the only judge and jury them four are gonna face. Besides, start doing a bunch of shooting in town and we're apt to get some innocent folks hurt.'

Tim looked long at the old man who sat across the fire from him. He had known Ezekiel Zimmerman for more than half of his own life. He had known him as a quiet man who usually kept to his own affairs. He and Antelope Horn had befriended and helped Tim's dad on more than one occasion and he and his dad had visited and hunted with the old men many times. He had lived there in the mountains with his good friend, Antelope Horn, and had been a peaceable man who never seemed to have had a harsh word for anyone. But now he was on the trail of Harding and his companions, kidnappers of Maggie Buckner and murderers of his long-time friend, partner and blood brother. He was a different man, now, deadly cold, methodical and an utterly relentless hunter. The man who now sat across the fire from him was one whom he did not recognize.

Tim knew that, had it not been for him, the old man would not have stopped to wait out the storm. Although the snow had gotten to be more than two feet deep the old man had trudged on like an old curly wolf stalking its prey. Tim realized that it was only when the old man had seen that he was succumbing to the bitter cold, that he had decided to seek shelter for a camp.

Now the young man reclined quietly near the fire listening to the wind, watching the occasional snowflake stray into the firelight under the overhang and thinking of what was to come. Suddenly he was thinking aloud. 'I've never killed a man.' His gaze quickly shifted from the snowflakes to the old man, who was relaxing with his coffee and snuff. 'I've never killed a man, Mr Zimmerman.'

At Tim's confession, the old man looked directly into the boy's eyes. There was iron in those dark-brown eyes, but there was innocence as well. What could he say? He had expected as much, but had never thought about addressing the subject. 'Well, Tim, it ain't an easy thing to do. I've seen growed men falter in battle when it come down to facing a man with a gun fer the first time — especially when that other feller were shooting back. You've hunted and killed game, but when ya kill an elk, say, the elk's just dead. But a man, now, that there's a whole different deal, a right serious deal. When ya pull the trigger on a man and take his life, you send him to meet his Maker; that's a heavy weight to shoulder. There ain't no shame in being afraid, or rather reluctant, to take a man's life.

'Now I don't know just how nervy

them boys are gonna be when lead starts flying around them. But I figure maybe only Alvin Harding hisself has the grit to face a man in a shooting scrape. He'd just figure gunning a feller would help to build his reputation. One of them others might be up to it, but I figure the majority of them'll probably hesitate a mite . . . and a mite's all the edge I'll need to get them all. When we go in on that bunch, your sole objective is to concentrate on getting to Maggie, getting her outta there and making sure she's safe. I'll do fer them four vermin myself.'

Tim stared into the fire for a few seconds then looked back up at the old man. 'I'm not afraid, Mr Zimmerman. I only meant that . . . well, I just want you to know that I'm not afraid, that's all.'

The old man smiled with his eyes and nodded. 'Never figured fer a minute that ya was, Tim. I know what you're saying though. Ya know, I might never have said this, but you've growed up to be right smart of a man, although I never had no doubt that you would.'

Tim smiled back at him. 'Thanks, Mr Zimmerman. I've had some pretty good examples to follow in Dad, Antelope Horn and you.'

In spite of his somber mood the old man chuckled. 'Well, sir, I ain't sure just how good of an example me and ole Horn have set fer ya, but I thank ya fer saying so.' Then he decided to ask the question that had been on his mind since the young man had joined him on Sheep Creek. 'Tim, what's the real reason ya come trailing after me? Oh, I reckon you figured I'd need some help sure enough, but maybe it had more to do with Maggie herself.'

Tim flushed with embarrassment as his lips formed a sheepish smile and he looked away from the old man and into the fire. 'We met a couple of days after she got to town and started spending time together almost immediately. You know, taking walks, having supper and sitting on the porch, even after the weather turned cold. I'd walk her and Mrs Oberman to and from church on the Sundays when the circuit rider made it to town and we went to the Easter social together and . . . well, other places. I guess I was sort of hoping that she would decide to stay in Casper permanently. I was hoping that, well . . . you know.' He stirred the fire with a long stick then added, 'Casper's a growing town. Dad's always saying that the railroad will eventually make it up that far. He guesses that it will more than likely put the stage line out of business, so we'll have to find another way to make a living. But, if that happens, land is cheap and I've saved a considerable amount of money. For several years he's talked about putting together a small cattle operation some-place close by and I was hoping that . . . well, maybe Maggie would stay in Casper, marry me and, with Dad's help, we'd build a small spread of our own.'

'Well, Tim, I reckon you'd make a

mighty good cattleman, but I always figured you fer a mountain man.'

Tim became excited at the notion of his ever being a mountain man. 'Oh, Mr Zimmerman! I love the mountains, more than any place I've ever seen; there's no place on earth like them. But I'm not sure there's enough beaver around nowadays to make a go of it and the buffalo are getting more scarce every day. I suppose, though, with a good season's trapping and hunting a fellow could make a good living; you and Antelope Horn have always done very well.'

The old man only nodded and nothing else was said. After the fire was banked for the night, each man retreated to his blankets and his own dreams. It was cold, very cold, and the old man lay close to the fire, feeling its warmth soak into his tired old muscles and aching hip. He suddenly thought of Maggie and hoped that she was warm . . . and unharmed.

11

Tim woke to the sound of the crackling of the fire and the smells of coffee, bacon and biscuits being prepared. It was still dark outside the shelter of the overhang, but he stirred slightly and the old man saw him move.

'Morning, Tim.'

Tim sat up and rubbed the sleep from his eyes, then he looked across the fire at the old man who was busy slicing more strips of salted pork from a slab and placing them in a skillet. 'Good morning, Mr Zimmerman. I'm sorry, but I guess I overslept.' He threw back his blankets and the top layer of his soogan, stood and eased closer to the fire. With his shoulders humped against the cold he scratched his head, took a deep breath and grunted a sigh. 'Uugh. What can I do to help?'

For the past couple of days the old

man had been melancholy and sullen. But after they had retired and he had rolled into his blankets, he had looked across the fire at the young man sleeping there and had reminisced about those days when Dub and Tim Combs had visited with him and Antelope Horn, sharing their fire while hunting. It had brought to mind many cheerful memories and he had slept peacefully and well. Perhaps that was the reason that on this morning he had awakened in a much lighter mood and was amused at the sleepy young man's eagerness to do his share of the chores. 'Well, sir, you can start getting the animals ready to travel. The weather's clearing off and the wind's coming up from the south-west this morning; we'll have a good day fer traveling. I'll give ya a hand with the horses just as soon as I get the rest of this bacon on.'

Tim walked to where the horses stood and began the task of brushing each, before laying the now dry saddle blankets over them. 'I guess it has stopped snowing, then.'

'Yep. Wind shifted early on. Snow turned to a light rain in the middle of the night, then quit altogether shortly thereafter. I reckon most of the snow out on the open ground will be gone by high sun, so it oughta be a good day fer us to cover some country.'

Neither man said anything for a while, as they saddled their horses. The old man was the one to break the silence. 'I reckon Harding will gether his supplies today. Tim, I know that I'm taking an awful gamble on which town they headed fer, but my gut just won't let me figure it no other way. He had to have took them to South Pass; that dang rope is the clincher.

'Now I don't figure them boys with him will be hankering to slope through no melting snow, so they'll probably spend another night in town — at least that's how I'm gonna figure it. That'll give us at least one full day to get ahead of them and set us up a place on high ground to watch fer them. I'm reckoning that they'll foller the Mormon Trail on across the Divide and on down to Bridger, 'cause them passes through the mountains will be snowed in, warmer weather or no. If they don't lollygag around, I reckon they'll leave South Pass in the morning, putting them at Pacific Springs by high sun. If he's asked them folks in South Pass any questions at all about the trail, he'll know that the best place to stop fer the night is where Pacific Creek joins the Big Sandy, west of Tule Butte; them wagon trains usually pull up in that neighborhood. He'll stop there all right, and that's where we'll catch up to them.'

Tim finished the saddling of the horses while the old man watched over their breakfast. Neither man talked while they ate, each deep in his own thoughts. Tim's thoughts were of Maggie and of the hardships that she had suffered over the past couple of years. She had told him the story of her father moving the family to South Dakota, of the death of her mother and of her being sold to Alvin Harding. Early in their relationship they had first talked of her plans for the future and then of his. He had gotten the feeling that little by little she had begun to have second thoughts about continuing on to Oregon; she had, over time, given him the impression that she wanted him to ask her to stay in Casper. He believed she would marry him, if he would only ask. But now his thoughts were only of her safety and that would mean the taking of the lives of Alvin Harding and his companions. Was he up to it? Could he take another man's life? He told himself that he could do whatever became necessary.

While Tim mulled over his thoughts of Maggie, the old man's mind covered the lay of the land around Tule Butte. Pacific Creek joined the Big Sandy only a couple of miles west of the tall mesa. He remembered a place on the western slope of the butte where he might observe the area around the confluence of the two streams and north back along the wagon trail for several miles. At that place he and Tim would watch the area with his long glass and wait. When Harding's group stopped for the night, and since Tim was present to slip in silently and remove Maggie from harm's way, he would close in. If all went as he had estimated, the chase would be over in the next couple of days, if, in fact, he was right and they had gone to South Pass. He forced himself not to think otherwise.

The sun was lifting its fiery, orange head above the Sweetwater Range as they rode away from the shelter of the Beaver Rim. The temperature was already rising and the warmth of the sun on their backs gave the two riders renewed energy, but for the first couple of hours, neither man had much to say as they made their way across the broken, rolling ground of the Great Divide.

On they rode throughout the day,

pausing only to allow their horses to drink at one of the occasional creeks or streams. The sun rose high overhead and the temperature along with it. As was the norm after a Wyoming spring blizzard, the warm south-west wind blew across the landscape as the temperature rose, so by mid-afternoon most of the snow on the open prairie had melted, leaving only patches of the frozen white liquid in the shaded areas. An hour before the sun dropped below the peaks of the Wasatch Range they stepped down within an outcropping of rocks high up on the western face of Tule Butte, nearly 1,100 feet above the prairie floor below. The sky was remarkably clear and the air was fresh after the passing of the storm. Even though the sun was going down, Tim was amazed at how far he could see; from their present position, spotting any travelers should be no problem at all.

Several times during the day, the old man had forced the thought, that he might have been mistaken about Harding's change of direction, to the back of his mind. He would not allow himself to start second guessing his decision. Many a war's been lost by second guessing one's battle plan, he had thought.

That night they made their camp, shielded by the rocks of the butte. As they relaxed around their small fire the old man drew Tim out regarding his plans for a cattle ranch. More than once he reminded the young man that there were several valleys and meadows in the area around Black Mountain, including the long valley through which Wolf Creek flowed, where cattle could be raised. He could think of no better people to have as his neighbors — if he must have neighbors.

★   ★   ★

The old man and Tim had ridden away from the Beaver Rim and had been in the saddle for nearly three hours, when

Alvin Harding rose on the morning after arriving in South Pass. When he looked out through the window, he saw that the storm had passed and the weather was improving rapidly. It was late morning when the group ate breakfast and again Maggie saw no one in the hotel dining room upon whom she could call for assistance. Then Arnold took her back to her room and Alvin, Jim and Sam gathered the supplies that they would need. Alvin purchased a horse and pack rig at the Black Horse Livery and enough supplies at one of the general stores to see them through to Salt Lake, in the event they were forced to detour from the trail or happened to by-pass Fort Bridger. Of course, their supplies included several bottles of whiskey.

That night, after once again threatening to cause a commotion large enough to attract the attention of everyone in the hotel, Maggie was allowed to go to bed without argument. However, once she was asleep, Alvin approached her and placed his hand over her mouth to muffle her screams. Maggie kicked frantically as her arms swung violently, striking him several times and she bit down hard on the hand that covered her mouth, forcing it to be withdrawn. But before she could scream for help, Alvin instantly swung his right hand in a blow that struck Maggie on the side of the head and then another, rendering her helpless in a semi-conscious state. When he had finished with her, Alvin stood over her and said, 'I told you that old man would never keep this from happening. Now, if you cause a commotion, I'll kill you.' Then he silently walked back to his bed, rolled into his blankets and fell asleep almost at once. Maggie lay on the bed sobbing and once more pulled the blankets over her. She wept until, finally, she cried herself to sleep.

Early the next morning Arnold and Sam brought their horses from the livery and tied them to a rail in front of the hotel. As they were preparing to leave South Pass City, a group of men, which included the town's marshal and a deputy, crossed the muddy street only a few yards away from where Harding and his group prepared to mount up. Seeing the only opportunity that she might have to obtain assistance to make her escape, Maggie suddenly and with all of her might jerked her arm from Alvin's grasp and bolted around the back of her horse. 'Help me, please! I've been abducted and am being forced to go with these men against my will!'

'Grab her, Arnold!' Alvin yelled, as he drew his six-gun. Arnold, who was between Maggie and the group of town's men, grabbed her as she attempted to run past him. Furiously she struggled to be free from his grasp, but Arnold was strong, despite his size, and was able to subdue her long enough to carry her back to her horse. Still she fought him, but he swung a fist, striking her on the left jaw and she crumpled to the ground unconcious.

As Alvin, Jim and Sam blasted away

at the marshal's group, Arnold lifted Maggie from the ground, slung her over his saddle, then stepped up, drew his pistol and spurred his mount past the marshal and his men, who had begun to return their fire. Two men of the marshal's group had already fallen under the onslaught of bullets fired by the men on horseback, as curious on-lookers filed on to the sidewalks and into the street. Bullets whizzed past Harding and his men as they blasted away at the marshal's group and the sulfurous, acrid smell of gunsmoke filled the air as they galloped down the street past the livery and out of town. Hoping to discourage any would-be pursuers, Alvin reined up at the top of the ridge with his Winchester in his hands, spun his horse to face the town and emptied the rifle, firing at anyone who ventured into the street and showed himself. Once he was relatively certain that no one would soon follow, he reined his big bay in the direction the others had ridden and followed after them.

Arnold had stopped in a small cottonwood grove just over a mile from the top of the ridge where Alvin had fired his rifle. Jim Emerson was tucking a wadded bandanna inside his shirt to stop the bleeding where a bullet had grazed his ribs and Maggie was just regaining her senses when Alvin rejoined them. Reining his horse to a sliding halt, he leapt from his saddle, marched with rage in his eyes to Maggie and proceeded to slap her savagely several times. Having once again been slapped nearly senseless, Maggie tearfully collapsed to the ground. Alvin grabbed her by the arms, snatched her back to her feet to face him and shook her ruthlessly for several seconds. Finally, Arnold grabbed his brother by the arm. 'That's enough Alvin, she has to be able to ride. Besides, those citizens back there might decide to grow a backbone and come after us. Let's get mounted and light out of here. You can slap her some more tonight if you want to.'

Alvin shoved Maggie back to the ground and spun to face his brother. 'Get her on her horse,' he snarled. 'Tie her hands to the horn and her feet to the stirrups . . . and I mean tie her tight.' Then he turned back to Maggie, pointed his finger at her and screamed, 'I've had a bellyful of your nonsense. I warned you what would happen if you caused me any more trouble. The next time, I swear, I'll put a bullet in your brain.'

Maggie sobbed uncontrollably, but Arnold quickly lifted her to her feet and led her to her horse. After helping her into the saddle he bound her hands to the horn and her feet to the stirrups, although not so tightly as Alvin would have done himself. Then he did something that surprised Maggie even in her disoriented state; Arnold patted her gently on the arm, almost as if he empathized with her. She was still sobbing as they rode out of the grove toward the wagon trail.

All morning they rode; seldom did anyone speak. Maggie, in fear of rekindling Alvin's rage, rode silently saying nothing at all. Twice during the morning Alvin sent Sam back along their trail to watch for anyone from South Pass who might be pursuing them. They pushed their horses hard and a half-hour before noon they stopped at Pacific Springs. When Sam rejoined them with news that he had seen no one on their backtrail, Alvin gave thought to spending the night at the springs. But with several hours of daylight remaining, he decided to ride on and make their camp at the place of which the hostler had told him.

That afternoon Alvin was uncompromising in his pushing of the group to cover the miles of broken prairie, driving them until his three cohorts had became disgruntled and irritable. Finally reaching the western bank of Pacific Creek they followed it south until they reached the Big Sandy. With both eyes blackened, a swollen left cheek and lower lip, along with various other minor injuries, Maggie worked at preparing their meal while the others, after unsaddling their horses, sat around the fire drinking whiskey.

'Tonight, Maggie.' Alvin was already feeling the effects of the liquor and his words were slurred. 'Tonight I'm going to beat you into submission again. Again . . . tonight . . . Maggie.'

As she worked preparing their food Maggie wept and prayed silently. 'Dear God, please help me. If You won't allow me to be freed . . . please, allow me to die.'

* * *

Harding and his men were shooting their way out of South Pass City as the two men high up on the side of Tule Butte finished their breakfast. Although it was still early morning, the old man was antsy as he and Tim began their watch. 'Watch close, Tim boy. We're about two and a half miles from where them streams join up; you can see the trees along the banks, as plain as can be. They'll probably be holding right close to the creek, so they're apt be a mite difficult to spot right off. It'll be something like watching fer an elk in the heavy timber, all you might get at first is a glimpse.' He had more instructions for Tim, but the old man stopped suddenly. He had spoken rapidly; he was nervous and he knew that Tim could see it in him. All through the previous night he had been troubled by that small voice in the back of his mind, which kept telling him that he had been mistaken about Harding's route. But he couldn't be wrong, he simply couldn't be. Maggie's wellbeing depended upon his being right. He stopped talking, collected himself, then looked over at Tim and chuckled softly. 'But what am I telling you fer? I've hunted with you before, Tim boy, you know what to look fer.'

Tim only smiled and nodded, then took the long glass and found a comfortable place to sit out his watch. The day passed slowly as he and the old man alternated two-hour watches. It was late afternoon and Tim had been watching a large herd of pronghorn antelope that were grazing some distance to the north, when he swung the long glass back in the direction of the creeks. The sweep he made was quick, but, as he swung past an area of sparsely wooded high ground along the western bank of the creek, he saw movement. Slowly, methodically he surveyed the ground over which he had just scanned and there, riding among the trees on the banks of Pacific Creek, near the mouth of Morrow Creek, he saw them.

'They're here! They're here, Mr Zimmerman.'

The old man hurried to Tim's side, squatted and took the long glass. 'Where?'

Tim pointed toward the place where he had seen the five riders. The old man raised the long glass to his eye and within seconds he too had located them. He breathed a long slow sigh of relief and quietly whispered a prayer of thanks. Then he stood and looked down at Tim. 'Saddle up, Tim. It's time to get this dance started.'

12

The old man led the way as they followed an ancient game trail down the west face of Tule Butte. He knew very well the lay of the land where Harding and his group would make their camp, so all that day he had drilled the young, inexperienced Tim regarding his plan of attack, going over it again and again with the young man. Hoping to permeate his mind with the pictures of how the plan must be carried out, he attempted to discuss in detail every possible scenario with which they might be faced. Now, once again, they rode in silence.

As he rode quietly Tim played each scenario in his mind and then replayed again. They had formed their battle plan, but there were a multitude of variables that might force a change in those plans, either during their approach or in the middle of the battle itself. To expect the four men to want to surrender peacefully was not even considered, nor, he knew, would the old man allow them to.

Tim had known the old man since he himself had been only a child. In all of those years he would never have believed that Ezekiel Zimmerman would hunt down a man for the sole purpose of killing him in cold blood, but he believed it now. Yet he lost no respect for him because of it, for he himself had similar feelings. There was a hot, burning fire of hatred and revenge in those steely old eyes and Tim knew that there would be no calming the rage inside his companion, even if he had wanted to.

Slowly, carefully they descended the mountain along the steep trail. With each step his horse took they came closer to a reckoning and the answer to the most crucial question ever asked of him. Tim could see more antelope grazing on the open prairie a mile or so south of where he now rode. Many times he had listened while his dad and the old man had talked philosophy over a camp-fire, but he was caught completely by surprise when, out of nowhere, a thought suddenly came to him: how simple the life of the wild animals.

It took nearly an hour to reach the base of the mountain. Once again being on the prairie floor, the old man turned the grulla's head toward the place where the Big Sandy and Pacific Creek came together. Slowly they rode across the broken, rolling terrain and still neither man spoke.

Tim had been praying that Maggie was unharmed and for the strength and courage to do what he knew would have to be done. He was deep in thought when he glanced beside him at the old man riding the pale-blue grulla. Suddenly he remembered hearing a passage from the Bible, when he was only a boy of eleven; a passage that, when the circuit rider had quoted it as he preached his sermon had for some reason frightened him. It was from the

187

book of Revelation and spoke of the end of time and of 'the judgement' . . . and of four horses and the 'beasts' who rode upon them. The first horse was white and ridden by the beast called Pestilence; the second was red and ridden by War. Third came a black horse ridden by the beast, Famine, and finally, there was a pale horse whose rider was Death. As he looked at the old man, in his mind's eye, he saw the frightening picture of those first three horsemen . . . and the old man and grulla were there with them as the fourth. And surely Hell followed close behind him.

* * *

Despite Alvin's drunken threats, Maggie soon had a fire going and the coffee pot was placed on a rock at its edge. As the old man and Tim walked their horses across the prairie toward the camp, she prepared their meal and prayed. The four men lounged near the fire, as Jim,

Arnold and Sam talked.

The sun had already disappeared below the peaks of the Wasatch Range as they spooned large helpings of beef, beans and fried potatoes onto their plates. The three younger men chatted casually as they ate, as if they had not a care in the world. But Alvin silently stared through glazed, empty eyes into the fire while he unconsciously forked-up mouthful after mouthful of the food; further evidence of his cousin Ben's assumption that Alvin was indeed insane. When he had finished his meal, he thoughtlessly tossed the tin plate to the ground near the fire, but he neither spoke a word nor altered his glare. Maggie and his three comrades glanced in his direction, but refrained from attempting to converse with him.

Maggie was hungry and wanted very much to eat, but she was terrified and her insides were tied in knots. After Alvin had beaten her earlier that day, she had prayed for death to take her. He had said that he would have her again this night and that if she gave him any argument he would beat her. But she swore to herself that she would never submit willingly. I'm at my rope's end, she thought as she looked at her food. If he comes after me again tonight, I'll fight and claw until he kills me, but I'll never just give in to him. Finally, she sat her still half-filled plate on the ground, walked to the southern edge of the camp and spread her bedroll along the length of an old seasoned log, as many other travelers had done before her. When she had rolled into her blankets, she slightly opened one eye to look back at Alvin; he had not moved. She breathed a tentative sigh of relief as once more she prayed silently for freedom, or for death. Then she closed both eyes and attempted to sleep.

Arnold, Jim and Sam continued to eat as they talked of their plans once having reached California. When they had finished eating, Jim cleaned the wound on his side while they talked;

cattle was the main topic of his and Arnold's portion of the conversation. But they were surprised when Sam spoke of his aspirations of having his own vineyard and winery. His family had been farmers in southwestern Pennsylvania and he had enjoyed the labors of bringing things to life and seeing them grow to be harvested. But he had idolized his older brother Tom, who had grown restless and wanted nothing more than to be away from what he had called, the backbreaking drudgery of farming. So when Tom had decided to leave Pennsylvania and head West, Sam had reluctantly joined him.

The three men talked for only a short time after they had finished eating. After having participated in a running gunfight to escape capture in South Pass and a day of hard riding, all three were exhausted, so they went to their blankets a short time after Maggie left the fire. Only Alvin remained near the fire into which he continued his blank, empty, mindless stare.

191

* * *

As darkness settled over the Great Divide, the old man and Tim swung south for a couple of miles, then turned north-west and again rode side by side for some time. Suddenly, Tim caught the scent of smoke from their fire and reined his mount to a halt. The old man had not smelled the smoke, but when Tim informed him of its presence he smiled with admiration at the young man's skill. He nodded to his young companion and stepped down from his saddle; Tim did likewise. Each man hobbled his horse, then retrieved his long gun from its scabbard; the old man carried his Henry, Tim's hands held a coach gun.

From where they had dismounted and left their horses, they walked only a short distance before hearing the running of water in the creek. Squatting in the darkness under the trees along the east bank of Pacific Creek the old man whispered his final instructions to

Tim, ' . . . and remember, your sole objective is to locate Maggie and a position where you can get to her fast. Signal when you're ready, then get her the heck out of there and to safety. Don't you worry about nothing else. There's gonna be a good bit of shooting, but that's fer me to worry about. You just get that girl outta there and make sure that, if they should get past me, they don't get her back. Fire only in defense of her or yourself. Once the fighting's over, I'll catch up to y'all.'

Tim responded affirmatively, then both rose and each man went his own way, Tim circling toward the southern edge of the camp, the old man to the north along the creek bank. When he was directly across the creek from the camp, the old man slipped ghostlike into the swift flowing stream and silently waded across in the icy knee-deep water. Then he slowly and quietly crawled up the opposite bank, finally stopping at the top behind a wide stump, which had long ago been shared by a pair of cottonwood trees. Now he had only to wait for Tim to get into position.

The old man surveyed the camp while he waited. As he slid into position behind the stump only the four men were in sight, three of them he could hear softly talking about their plans for the future. After a quick search, he found Maggie rolled into her blankets near an old log. Before Tim could signal that he was in position, the three younger men rose and walked to their bedrolls leaving only Alvin Harding seated near the fire.

They ain't too smart, the old man thought as he positioned the Henry in the fork of the stump. Them boys have been looking into that fire. They couldn't see a herd of buffalo walking out here in the dark if their lives depended on it. And soon, very soon, it would. Now he waited for Tim.

As he awaited the signal that would launch the attack on the camp, the old man relaxed, slowing and controlling his breathing, calming himself so that he would not shoot too quickly; he must make each shot count. When the signal finally came, he was calm and ready.

It was a low, soft owl hoot, which came from only a few yards south-west of where Maggie lay, that he heard causing him to lay his cheek along the stock of the rifle and take aim at the man seated on the log only a few yards away. He had no qualms about shooting the man in the back — front or back, he simply wanted him dead. Slowly, he took up the slack in the trigger. Time to play some music and get this ball started, he thought.

With its sights set between Harding's shoulder blades the Henry belched flame and roared its deadly tune. Quickly the old man operated the lever and fired into Harding again. Time and his old hip wound had taken their toll on him physically, but instinctively he rolled to his left, coming up behind the thick trunk of another tree. Harding had jerked violently with the impact of the first bullet and had sprung to his feet, but was spun by the second and had fallen to the ground a few feet away, on the opposite side of the fire from where he had sat.

The old man operated the lever quickly and fired two rapid shots into Jim Emerson, who, although he could not see well after having been looking into the fire, was on one knee and firing the Colt in his hand. Of the two shots fired at Emerson, one slug struck him in the chest, passed through his body and broke his back. The other entered his throat and broke his neck, killing him instantly.

Instinctively, the old man had chambered another round and he fired into young Sam Ferguson, who had thrown back his blankets with the first shot and had rolled to his knees with no weapon in his hand. Ferguson was frantically running his hands over the ground searching for his Colt when the .44 slug struck him under the right armpit, passed through his body and exited just under his left collarbone. For young Sam there would be no vineyard, no winery . . . in fact, Sam Ferguson had no future at all. As he lay face down in the dirt, his hand only inches from his six-gun, young Sam breathed his last and died.

The old man rolled again, then allowed himself a quick glance in the direction of Maggie's bed, but she was no longer there; he could only hope that Tim had succeeded in carrying out his assignment and that she had gotten safely away. Seeing that Maggie was no longer in the camp, he returned his attention to the gunplay at hand.

Immediately he saw that Arnold Harding's bedroll was empty. He was nowhere in sight and the old man cursed himself for a fool. He should never have taken the time to look for Maggie, but depended upon Tim's knowledge and skill to enable him to fulfill his task and see her to safety. He was still silently rebuking himself when there came a shotgun blast from a short distance away on his left, south of the camp. Immediately, there came a second blast and that area of the small grove was lighted by the flames that belched from the shotgun's muzzle. Then, all was silent. Just as suddenly as it had begun, only a few seconds before, the shooting ended.

For several minutes the only sounds that could be heard were the crackling of the fire, the rustling of the leaves and the gentle, soft, gurgling sounds made by the water as it flowed over the rocks, making its way down Pacific Creek. Even the night sounds of the crickets and frogs had been silenced. He continued listening to the water and smiled as he thought about the snow on the mountains that melted and passed between the banks of the creek behind him, eventually flowing into the Pacific Ocean. Why he had smiled at the thought, or even had the thought at all, he had no idea. Perhaps it was the philosopher within him.

Finally the old man slowly stood, but still remained concealed by standing close to the trunk of a nearby tree, his eyes searching for any movement. Several more minutes passed before he was confident enough that the recipients of his wrath had indeed met their uninvited demise and he stepped quietly to the edge of the camp. There, he waited again.

He finally took a step toward Alvin Harding, whose body lay closest to him, and out of the corner of his eye he saw movement. Glancing in the direction of that movement as the Henry came up, he saw Tim approaching the log near which Maggie had lain; the girl was only a couple of steps behind him. They had both moved silently and only when they had advanced into the flickering light of the dwindling fire did he know that they were there. He once again lowered the rifle, but held it ready.

'Either of ya injured?' Neither reported any wounds. 'You two'll do to ride the river with,' he praised with a smile. They were smiling back at him and Maggie's lips were forming a word in reply, when there was the thundering blast of another gunshot. Instantly, he felt the fruit of its application and his knees buckled.

As the old man slumped to the ground, Tim was already leaping over the log and the shotgun once again bellowed as flames erupted from its muzzle; Maggie raced to the old man's side. Tim walked a step closer to Alvin Harding and fired the load of buckshot from the second barrel into him; *now*, Alvin Harding was dead. Then he checked the other two bodies to make certain of them.

The first wound near Harding's spine had been severe and had instantly numbed his legs and right arm, although he had somehow been able to stand. The old man's second shot had struck him high and right, and the shock of that second slug had knocked him senseless. For a few seconds, as he lay on the ground, his surroundings had spun, he had been dizzy and sick, then he had blacked out.

But as the old man had stood at the edge of the camp, Harding had regained consciousness. Through the fogginess and the buzzing in his head, he had discovered that he still had some feeling in his left arm and hand. When the old man had spoken to the two young people, his attention had been diverted away from Harding, who had lifted his Colt with an unsteady left hand and had fired into him. He was attempting to thumb back the hammer for another shot when Tim's first load of buckshot had struck him in the chest . . . the second load of .30 caliber-sized lead pellets had not been needed, for Harding had been killed instantly by the first.

When Tim finished his inspection of Sam Ferguson and Jim Emerson's bodies he checked Alvin once more. When he turned away from Harding's bloody, shot-riddled body, he found Maggie seated on the ground with the old man's head in her lap. As he stood over them the old man opened his eyes and looked up at him. 'You get him, Tim?'

'Yes, sir, I got him, Mr Zimmerman. It's all over.'

'Yes, sir, it is. You done real good, Tim boy. Thank ya, son, from me and ole Horn.' The old man lay quietly for a few seconds, then said, 'Now, there ain't no need for the two of you to hang around here, so be on your way. Maggie's gotta get back yonder to gether up her truck and catch that stage fer Oregon . . . if she's still of a mind to go. And Tim, your folks'll be worrying about you. I reckon I'll just lay here a while. I'm feeling a bit used up.'

'No, Mr Zimmerman, we'll not leave you,' Maggie cried out. 'Tim can make a travois and we'll take you to South Pass City. We'll find a doctor there. He'll patch you up and I'll nurse you back to health.'

Through the pain that was now beginning to take hold of his insides the old man reached around and from his back he brought back his hand covered with blood. He held the bloody hand out and looked up at Tim, 'My eyes ain't working so good. What color's the blood, Tim?'

Tim blinked several time to clear away the tears, then shook his head and answered with trembling lips, 'It's dark red, sir.'

'It's all right, boy.' He closed his eyes and groaned. 'Maggie girl, I don't reckon there's any use trying to get me to that doctor. But if you fellers wanta wait with me here fer a little while, I don't reckon I'll mind none. Mornin'll be soon enough fer ya to head back to Casper.' Maggie fiercely protested, but Tim placed his hand on her shoulder and she, too, knew that attempting to get the old man to a doctor would be to no avail. She simply lowered her head and sobbed. They packed the wound in an effort to stop the bleeding and made the old man as comfortable as possible, then they waited there with him.

Maggie cradled his head, caressed his

bearded cheeks and softly ran her fingers over his bald head and through his long white hair. Tim added fuel to the fire and started a fresh pot of coffee. For hours they waited. Several times the old man groaned softly from the pain and each time Maggie held his hand. Twice during the night he awoke. The first time he only smiled, patted Maggie on the arm and then drifted off once more. The second time he looked over at Tim, who had fallen asleep near the fire as he leaned against one of the logs there. 'Tim's a good man, Maggie girl.'

But she was irritated with Tim. 'Oh, I can't believe he fell asleep. There's no way on earth — '

'I'd been more surprised if he hadn't,' the old man interrupted weakly. 'A feller gets all het-up in a shooting skirmish like we's in. The adrenaline starts pumping and ya just keep on fighting without thinking nor tiring; a feller gets wounded and sometimes don't even know it 'til later. But when it's all over and done with and the adrenaline's all used up, a body gets mighty tired . . . downright weak. I've done the same thing before myself, several times. Just collapsed on my bunk afterwards.

'Maggie, I want ya to tell Tim . . . ' He gripped her hand tightly and winced from the pain. When the pain had subsided he relaxed again. 'Well, I reckon I'll just rest a while, before I make that trip to meet up with ole Horn. I reckon he'll play hob over me not checking on my quarry to make sure he was finished, just like I done over that ole elk what gored him.' He chuckled softly, then added, 'Take care of yourself, Maggie, and tell that young feller yonder to do the same.' Having said that, the old man closed his eyes and once again slept, or passed out. Maggie couldn't have said which it was.

The sky had already turned gray and the orange glow of the sun was appearing over the Divide when, without having spoken again and with both of the young people at his side, the old man sighed softly and relaxed with the peace of death. Maggie sobbed sorrowfully, while Tim attempted to comfort her, as he wept along with her.

Tim tied lead ropes to the horses of Harding and his men, then led the grulla into the camp. After wrapping the old man's body in his slicker, he gently draped him across his saddle and tied him down. Then he and Maggie mounted, gathered the lead ropes of the other horses and crossed Pacific Creek, heading toward the rising sun and home. The bodies of Alvin and Arnold Harding, Jim Emerson and Sam Ferguson lay where they had fallen.

13

It took over four days to get back to Casper. The street became crowded as the town's residents, as well as a few who were just passers-through, stopped and stared as Tim and Maggie walked their small herd of horses through the town to the stage station. As they both stepped down, Dub Combs stepped from the station to greet them. When he saw the body, wrapped and draped over the saddle on the grulla, he shook his head and sighed sadly, 'Oh, Dutchman.'

Tim walked to the stable while his dad stepped back inside the station. Maggie stood near the hitch-rail holding the reins of the grulla. In only a few seconds both men returned to the horses, Tim with a pick and shovel, his dad carrying his Bible. Maggie led the tall blue grulla as the three walked silently to the cemetery, where Tim dug the grave in which the old man was to be laid to rest. It was under a tall pine tree next to his longtime friend, the Sioux warrior Antelope Horn.

As Tim and his dad lowered the wrapped body of Ezekiel Zimmerman into the grave, Laura Oberman and Tim's mother, Octavia, approached the graveside. Dub Combs presided over the emotional ceremony by reading the old man's favorite passage from his Bible and then saying a few words about his dear old friend. After the grave was covered, the five attendees walked somberly back to the stage station, where Tim led the grulla to the stable and turned him into the corral with Antelope Horn's paint and their pack horse.

When Tim entered the house he found his dad and Laura Oberman seated at the kitchen table while his mother and Maggie prepared coffee and food for all five of them. He and Maggie told in detail the perilous story of her captivity, of her draping the lariat over the snow-covered sagebrush and the gun battle to escape South Pass City. Then they described the tracking and locating of Harding's group and of the eventual, successful yet tragic outcome. Electing to keep the incident her secret, Maggie never mentioned being assaulted in the hotel room.

When the discussion of the story had slowed, from her purse Laura Oberman produced a leather-wrapped bundle and an envelope which she handed to Tim. 'Mr Zimmerman left the leather bundle with me four years ago; the envelope he gave to me on that first day they came into town . . . the day before Maggie was abducted. He told me that when the time came that he and Antelope Horn had passed on, I was to give this to you, Tim. I've never opened it, so I do not know what it holds, although I have my suspicions.'

While the others waited patiently, Tim untied its bindings then rolled out the bundle, revealing a number of papers. Among them were the old man's Last Will & Testament, the deed to the homestead on which the cabin was built, a few other legal documents and a letter that explained them all. Then, with tears in his eyes, he opened the envelope which contained another letter and a thousand dollars in paper money.

Tim wiped away the tears with his shirt sleeve, then read aloud the letter from the envelope which said:

Dear Tim

If you're reading this letter, then me and ole Horn have gone to those happy hunting grounds in the hereafter. Please thank Mrs Oberman for me, for seeing after these papers. She's been a good friend to us.

Tim, I never had a son and ole Horn lost his only son many years ago. We both enjoyed those times when we put our feet under your family's table during our visits to Casper. We both especially enjoyed the times when you and Dub came to visit us there in our valley east of Black Mountain and those days spent hunting in the mountains we all love so. We watched you grow into a man, honest and strong, gaining in skills and ability to hunt and make your mark on wild country. Both of us would have been proud to have called you Son. That being said, you now own ALL that belonged to me and ole Horn.

Dub has talked for years of someday owning enough land for the raising of cattle. Although it is at a high elevation, I believe the area around Black Mountain to be well suited for such a purpose. Grass and water are abundant, and you are a capable man.

You had been the only youngster in our lives until Maggie came along last year. I reckon, although we didn't deserve it, the Good Lord was being kind to the two of us old men as well as to her, for in just a very short time we came to feel for her as we would have a daughter.

As I sat down to write this letter, Mrs. Oberman was telling me that you and Maggie have been keeping time while she has lived in Casper. If, when you read this letter, she is still here and the two of you are married or are to be married, our hopes have been fulfilled. She will share in your dreams and the land left to you. I do believe she enjoyed her time there with us.

If she has left Casper and continued her trip to her people in Oregon, see that she gets this money. Used wisely, it is enough to help her make her future out there without having to depend on anyone else for support. I believe she said they owned a farm near Ashland, Oregon.

Me and Horn wanted to help her, but she refused to accept money from us. Tell her I said that it ain't charity, it's a gift and a feller has a right to give a gift to a friend.

You and your family have been a

pleasure to know. Your folks are GOOD people and you should treasure them. Please give them my fondest regards.

Live a long and happy life, Timmy boy. You have a good heart and soul. We believe you'll do well.

WE have been proud to call you FRIEND.Sincerely,
Zeke

PS I almost forgot. Remember the loose stones.

Through tear-filled eyes, Tim looked up from his seat at the end of the table to see that the others were sniffing and wiping away tears as well.

★   ★   ★

Two weeks after returning to Casper, with her year's savings and the money left to her by the old man and Antelope Horn, Maggie Buckner boarded the stage bound for Salt Lake. Tim had used all of his powers of persuasion to convince her to stay and become his wife. Each time they talked, both would leave their meeting saddened and Maggie would be in tears. Tim could not understand her sudden change of heart; Maggie could not bring herself to tell him of the incident in South Pass City. In the end, she tearfully boarded the coach, crossed the bridge for the last time and rolled out of his life forever. From the door of the station Tim watched the coach sadly, until it was out of sight.

The following morning, he crossed that same bridge and rode north, toward the Big Horns, leading the grulla and paint, both carrying supplies; there was much he needed to do. At high sun on the third day after leaving Casper, he dismounted near the door of the cabin east of Black Mountain. He found that the garden had already been planted before the old man and Antelope Horn had left for Casper. Although the entire garden was in need of some weeding, the corn, beans, cabbage, potatoes and squash had already sprouted; he would have those much needed vegetables after all.

After turning his horse into the corral, he removed the packs and saddles from the grulla and the paint then led them away from the cabin past the stream that flowed from the waterfall pool. There he removed the bridle from both, slapped the grulla on the rump and watched them trot off into the timber. They were both superb mounts, but the old man and his companion were gone and he could not bring himself to ride either of their horses. Although he knew that they would have wanted him to use them, somehow, he knew that he never could.

When Tim finally got around to checking the 'loose stones' to which the old man had referred in his letter, he found over $4,000 in gold coins and paper money and a map drawn on a leather hide.

When he had read the folded leather

map, he left the cabin carrying an oil lamp, walked around the west side of the house and entered the cave. After moving a few of the crocks of sauerkraut and a wooden bin that held potatoes, he was able to make his way to the back wall of the vegetable cellar. Tears filled his eyes when he found the impressively large deposit of rich jade.

He replaced the potato bin and crocks, then walked out into the sunlight at the entrance of the cave. There he pulled the map from his shirt pocket and read the words written at the bottom of the skin:

Tim,

Laura Oberman has always been my agent in the selling of my stones, so that we could keep the deposit a secret. I have spoken to her on this matter and she has agreed to do the same for you. You can trust her. Sell only a small amount at a time as needed, so as not to drive the price down. It is high-grade jade, but use it sparingly and wisely. It should keep you going when times are hard.

Dutchman

He walked around to the front of the house and took a seat on the split log, which served as a bench, near the door. From there he could see nearly the entire valley. It was a beautiful setting and he had always loved this place. A couple of the horses, which had been released by the old man when he and Antelope Horn had left for Casper, were grazing far down on the lower end of the valley; the other animals, Tim was certain, would be close by. Although he had noticed a few loose chicken feathers lying on the ground near the chicken house, several of the hens and one old rooster were pecking and scratching in the dirt a few yards from the barn.

He pulled a tin box from his pocket, took out a pinch of the finely chopped tobacco that it held and placed it between his lower lip and gum. As he relaxed against the front wall of the cabin, he again looked down the valley at the straying animals and thought about the things he would do.

Tomorrow he would gather all of the straying animals and, if time allowed, begin the task of hoeing the weeds from the garden. For the rest of the summer he would cut and gather the tall grass of the valley for hay. When the vegetables were ready to be harvested he would, as had been done for so many years before, gather them, then haul them to the cave for storage.

Although there remained several large bales of furs in the cabin, including most of those from the previous winter's trapping, he would trap during the coming winter and gather more furs and hides, as his friends had done before him. He would also do what he could to gather timbers for another barn; a barn that would be needed when his parents arrived in the spring with the first of the cattle.

His friends had made a good life for

themselves and lived a comfortable life here in this special place among the Big Horns and in their generosity they had left it to him. Now, he would make *his* life and future here in this beautiful valley east of Black Mountain.

THE END

We do hope that you have enjoyed reading this large print book.

Did you know that all of our titles are available for purchase?

We publish a wide range of high quality large print books including:
Romances, Mysteries, Classics
General Fiction
Non Fiction and Westerns

Special interest titles available in large print are:
The Little Oxford Dictionary
Music Book, Song Book
Hymn Book, Service Book

Also available from us courtesy of Oxford University Press:
Young Readers' Dictionary
(large print edition)
Young Readers' Thesaurus
(large print edition)

For further information or a free brochure, please contact us at:
Ulverscroft Large Print Books Ltd.,
The Green, Bradgate Road, Anstey,
Leicester, LE7 7FU, England.
Tel: (00 44) **0116 236 4325**
Fax: (00 44) **0116 234 0205**

HIDEOUT AT MENDER'S CROSSING

John Glasby

The ghost town of Mender's Crossing is the ideal base for a gang of outlaws operating without interference. When a group of soldiers is killed defending a gold-train, the army calls upon special operator Steve Landers to investigate. However, Landers is also up against land baron Hal Clegg: his hired mercenaries are driving independent ranchers from their land. He will need nerves of steel to succeed when he is so heavily outnumbered. Can he cheat the odds and win?

DEAD MAN RIDING

Lance Howard

Two years ago Logan Priest left the woman he loved to shelter her from the dangers of his profession . . . but he made a terrible mistake. A vicious outlaw whom he brought to justice escapes prison and seeks revenge on the very woman that Priest had sought to protect. Logan is forced to return to the manhunting trail when he receives the outlaw's grisly calling card. Can he meet the challenge, or will he become the killer's next victim?

FIGHTBACK

Joseph John McGraw

When Tom Harker gets shot at, there's nothing personal about it, but when he shoots back, things change . . . Walter Viall, the cattle king of Tate Country, has a murky past and doesn't take kindly to strangers meddling in his affairs. He has used intimidation and violence to get the law-abiding town of Laureston exactly where he wants it — and he has no intention of letting anyone get in his way. He remains unchallenged . . . until Tom leads the fightback . . .

RAILROAD TO REDEMPTION

I. J. Parnham

The influx of railroad men looking to build a new track to Redemption brings trouble for Sheriff Cassidy Yates. But when Dayton Fisher arrives, looking for work, things seem to be looking up. And his bravery persuades Luther to hire him as a bodyguard. However, when he also takes on gunslingers to cause mayhem about town, Luther is killed and suddenly Dayton is pitted against his friend Cassidy. Can the two men be reconciled and defeat the gunslingers?